BOBBY BRIGHT
SPENDS CHRISTMAS
IN SPAIN

BY

John R. Brooks

ILLUSTRATIONS BY
**Dan Daly, Troy Gustafson
and Jeff Elliott**

Published by Old Farm Press
P.O. Box 20894 | Oklahoma City, Oklahoma 73156 USA
1.405.748.7072 | www.bobbybrightbooks.com

Interior design by Lindsay B. Behrens
Illustration by Dan Daly, Troy Gustafson and Jeff Elliott

Published in the United States of America

ISBN: 978-1-61777-462-1
1. Juvenile Fiction / Holidays & Celebrations / Christmas & Advent
2. Juvenile Fiction / People & Places / Europe
16.11.11

Foreword

In Author John Brooks' first book, *Bobby Bright's Greatest Christmas*, we were introduced to Bobby, the world's first talking Christmas tree light bulb. Bobby decides to take action after his family Christmas tree light bulb strand has experienced the past ten years hanging from the back of the Christmas tree, unseen by his human family.

Bobby's powers grow in the second book of the series, *Bobby Bright's Christmas Heroics*. After a destructive tornado, he becomes a true hero, who saves the lives of not only two of his bulb strand family members, but also two of his human family members.

In *Bobby Bright Spends Christmas in Spain*, Bobby goes international! Through careful planning and pure luck, our resolute Christmas tree light bulb brings his family strand to Spain. In Mr. Brooks' third *Bobby Bright* series book, we will continue to experience Bobby's increasing abilities and powers as he and his friend Remington face startling challenges together.

As a fellow reader, teacher, and librarian, I highly recommend these hilarious books about the unusual adventures of a very extraordinary talking Christmas tree light bulb.

Vicky Horton Standridge
Language Arts Teacher and Library Media Specialist

Contents

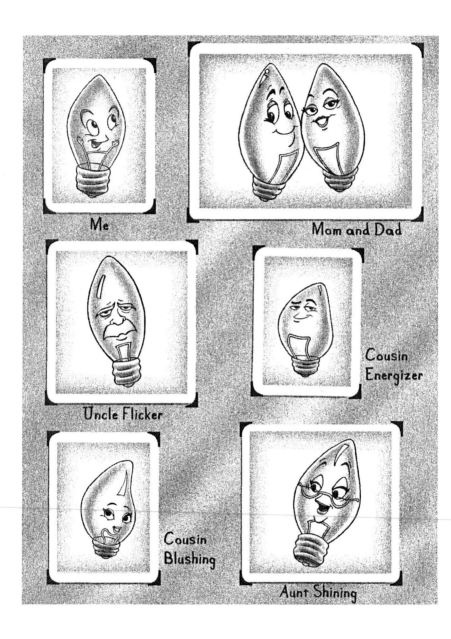

<u>Prologue</u>

Christmas Night Last Year

"**C**an't we stay a couple of more days like we did last year?" Remington asked his mom.

"We've been through this, Remington," she answered. "You know Daddy has to be back at work the day after tomorrow."

At that moment, Remington's grandfather walked into the room. "It's going to be real early in the morning when you have to leave, old buddy, so close those eyes and go to sleep."

"I know," Remington whined. "But I just wanted to look at my Christmas tree and all my beautiful bulbs a little bit longer." He reached up to give his grandfather a hug, and he started to cry.

"What's wrong, little guy?" Mr. McGillicuddy asked as he reached down and picked up his eight-year-old grandson.

Remington wiped a tear from his face and said, "It was just such a great Christmas, Grandpa. The food was good, especially the desserts, and the presents, and thank you again for the computer. You and Grandma surprised me."

"You bet we did," said Mrs. McGillicuddy as she walked into the guest room. This was the second straight

Christmas Remington had slept in the upstairs room with his very own Christmas tree.

"I hope you learned your lesson about peeking in closets, or anywhere for that matter, when you are told not to. Also, I hope you've learned never to jump on a bed. You are lucky you didn't have a terrible concussion from that fall to the floor."

"I'm sorry, Grandma. I learned my lesson, and thanks to my buddy, Bobby, I'm safe and sound."

"Please, Remy," his mom said and frowned at him, "don't keep trying to make us believe that bulb is magical."

Remington's dad laughed quietly as he listened to the conversation while standing in the doorway.

"I know you don't believe he can talk, but at least Grandpa does," said Remington, and his mouth quivered as if he might start crying.

"Oh, really, does he?" Mrs. McGillicuddy laughed. "Well, he's told me for months they saved me during the tornado. Who knows? Maybe it's true. There have been some mysterious things happening around here."

"I guess we better let Remington tell his Christmas tree light bulbs good night," said his dad, "so he can get to sleep."

"I'm going to miss being here at Christmas so much next year," Remington said as he leaped up into the arms of his grandmother and gave her a big hug.

"Remington!"

"What, Daddy?"

Before Remington's father could answer, Mrs. McGillicuddy said, "What do you mean by that, Remington?"

It was the next morning. Remington and his mom and dad were downstairs packing the SUV before their trip of more than a thousand miles to their home. Bobby heard them talking with the McGillicuddys. He lay at the front of the tiny tree, still having trouble believing what he had heard last night.

He remembered how shocked the bulbs in his family were when he had told them Mr. and Mrs. McGillicuddy were going to Spain next Christmas. There would be no need for a Christmas tree, and the bulbs would remain in the ornament box in the foyer closet.

It would be so different from the past two Christmas seasons. The first nine years at the McGillicuddys' house, the bulbs were never seen by anyone because each year they were at the back of the big Christmas tree downstairs. However, Bobby's magical powers had helped change all of that. The last two years had been wonderful. They had found a home on Remington's tiny Christmas tree in the upstairs bedroom.

Bobby's thoughts were interrupted by the voice of his favorite uncle, Flicker. "*I still can't believe this. You mean we are going to be stuck in that closet downstairs for almost two years?*"

"It sure seems that way," said Bobby.

"What is Spain?" asked Bobby's sister, Sparkle.

"It's a country, and it's across some ocean, and it's thousands of miles away. Remington's dad is going to be working at the United States embassy in Madrid, which is the capital city of Spain."

"Tell me again, Bobby. What exactly happened?"

"Dimmer, you are a wonderful brother, but sometimes you pay no attention. I'm not going to tell you the whole story."

"Oh, Bobby." His mom twisted in her pod and leaned against him. "Be nice to your brother. He's a blinking bulb. He takes longer to understand."

"All right, Dimmer, and anyone else who didn't pay attention, here's the story." Then Bobby told all of them again in their unique *Bulbese* language how Remington's mom and dad had bought airline tickets for the McGillicuddys to go to Spain. They would be staying three weeks with them in Madrid during the Christmas and New Year holidays.

And back in America, Bobby and his family would lie in a box in a dark closet, with no chance to do the one thing they did better than anything: shine and make people happy.

When Bobby had finished telling the story again, he heard his mom crying. Uncle Flicker bellowed, "This is unacceptable."

"Bobby, you have to do something. Why can't we go to Spain?" yelled Dimmer.

"I know you will find a way to do it, Bobby," his mom encouraged.

"Yeah, you will," said Dimmer. "In fact, brother, you are the man. You can save us. I know you can."

Next to him, in the pod to his left, Aunt Glaring twisted and leaned toward him. She clinked up against him and smiled. "You have eleven months to figure out a way to get us there. You'll think of something."

Bobby looked at her and winked. "I always do." And then the whole Bright family cheered loudly when he shouted, "Okay! Christmas in Spain."

Our Family Picture

PART ONE

1

Spring-Cleaning

For nearly four months, Bobby and his family waited for that annual time of the year when the box where they lived, filled with ornaments and light bulbs, would be brought out of the closet for the annual spring-cleaning period at the McGillicuddys' house. Bobby and his family would have a chance to see the light of day and escape the dungeon, which was the name they used to describe the closet.

In years past, it had made little difference because their strand of lights had always been at the bottom of the box. They couldn't see anything, except on very bright days, when a few rays of light would creep under the closet door and possibly be strong enough to reach the bottom of the box. But after last spring, when Bobby and his family's magical powers had helped save Mrs. McGillicuddy's life after a terrible tornado, the bulbs had ended up being placed at the very top of a new storage box.

During the past four months, Bobby had been able to clearly see light from underneath the closet door during daylight hours. Even so, the days still dragged by slowly, and for some reason, Bobby felt as if this was the longest they had ever waited for spring-cleaning during their eleven years at the McGillicuddys' house.

Bobby whispered to the other bulbs on the strand, *"I think it is cleaning time, everyone."* The bulbs started to cheer and chatter among themselves in their unique *Bulbese* language, but Bobby yelled, *"Be quiet! Let me make sure."*

He listened and heard Mr. McGillicuddy going up and down the hallway stairs as he ran errands for Mrs. McGillicuddy. Then Bobby suddenly whispered, *"Hold everything. I just heard Mr. McGillicuddy yell to Mrs. McGillicuddy that he's going to get the boxes out of the closet and put them in the foyer."*

But, within seconds, the closet door opened and Bobby saw Mrs. McGillicuddy instead. He was excited. If everything went as it normally did each year, the box would probably sit in the foyer for at least two days while the McGillicuddys cleaned every corner of their home.

Mrs. McGillicuddy liked cleaning the closet herself because she did a better job than her husband. She would run the vacuum cleaner over the floor two, three, and maybe even four times, before she was satisfied it was clean. And she would always dust every piece of clothing that hung on the racks. She took pride in doing everything right. It wasn't the same with Mr. McGillicuddy. He liked to find ways to get things done as quickly as possible, which normally meant he never cleaned anything as well as it should be.

The moment the door opened, Bobby knew Mrs. McGillicuddy meant business. She marched right into the closet and gave her husband instructions on where to put the boxes and what clothes she wanted removed from the closet. Then she told him she was thirsty and was going to go get a drink of water. "Have that finished when I get back, John."

Mr. McGillicuddy dragged the box of ornaments and lights into the foyer. He also pulled three old suitcases from the closet. He then loaded the clothes Mrs. McGillicuddy wanted moved into his arms and hurried out the door. A moment later, Mrs. McGillicuddy rounded the corner. "When you get done with those clothes, hurry back down here, John, because there are lots of sacks of trash to take to the curb."

She started up the vacuum cleaner. Inside the box it was noisy, and Bobby wondered how much louder it would sound if the box were still in the closet.

Mrs. McGillicuddy worked in the closet for over fifteen minutes, running the noisy vacuum cleaner, and dusting off the clothes that hung inside. When she finished, she called for Mr. McGillicuddy but didn't get an answer. She paused for a moment and then strode out of the foyer. "I bet he's outside on the patio, stretched out on that lounge chair, and taking a nap."

When Bobby heard her open the door to the patio, he translated to the other bulbs what she had said. Then all of the bulbs laughed, as they always did when they heard stories about Mr. McGillicuddy.

"The goofiest guy in the world," said Aunt Glaring.

"And the biggest doofus anywhere," yelled Bobby's brother, Dimmer.

The bulbs laughed but Bobby sat staring into space. *"What is it, Bobby?"*

"You know, Mom, I've been thinking. I need to be more serious. I've got to come up with a plan soon, or we are going to be locked in that closet for another year."

"I know, Bobby. You've got to figure out a way to get us to Spain."

Bobby had spent most of the last four months in the darkness of the closet and still hadn't figured out how he could do it. But little did he know, he would find the answer in less than a day.

2
Working on the Plan

There were way too many things left to do on the long list of chores Mrs. McGillicuddy had put together for this year's spring-cleaning. That meant the box with the bulbs, along with other items from the closet would remain in the foyer for the night.

The bulbs enjoyed their chance to be free and see something more than the shadows of the clothes hanging above them in the closet.

After chattering away in *Bulbese* after the McGillicuddys had gone to bed, the bulbs finally became tired and went to sleep. Only Bobby remained awake. He kept thinking of an idea he had thought of to get the bulbs to Spain. He had mentioned it to his mom, who had said, "*As crazy as it sounds, it might be possible. Only you could make it happen.*"

As he lay awake in the foyer, the idea still sounded crazy. However, he didn't know what Mr. McGillicuddy was about to do later that morning.

The alarm had gone off at seven o'clock. Mr. McGillicuddy quickly headed to the shower and Mrs. McGillicuddy to the kitchen. Twenty minutes later, Mr. McGillicuddy was sitting at the table, and Mrs. McGillicuddy was placing toast, two eggs, and three paddies of sausage on his plate.

"Why did you go take that shower, John? I've got so much for you to do that you will be dirty by 8:30. Then you will need another shower."

"I thought you said we had everything done."

"No, dear," Mrs. McGillicuddy answered and pulled up a chair next to him. She sat down to drink a cup of coffee. "I said we were close to having everything finished. We still have the garage to do."

"No, Jane, please! Not the garage. I'm not in the mood."

"I'm never in the mood for the garage either because there is too much junk in it," she answered, "but that is why we are going to round up all the little items we don't need and either put them in the trash or send them to Goodwill."

Mr. McGillicuddy spent the next ten minutes slowly eating his sausage and eggs. He would have taken longer if he could, but Mrs. McGillicuddy made him hurry and finish breakfast. She wanted him to start moving all of that junk, as she liked to call it, out of the garage and into the driveway. Then they would make some decisions on what to keep and throw away.

After breakfast, Mrs. McGillicuddy spent fifteen minutes washing the dishes and cleaning up the kitchen. Then she opened the door to the garage and looked to see if Mr. McGillicuddy was working. She didn't see him immediately and said loudly, "John, where are you? What are you doing?"

When there was no answer, she stepped into the garage and walked around the car to the opposite side. Then she saw him. He was swaying back and forth and shaking his hips as he stared out the back window of the garage. "What are you doing?" she yelled, but he didn't answer.

He was wearing a small headset plugged into an old cassette recorder that was clipped to his belt. She began to laugh, and then she laughed some more when he began clapping his hands over his head. His hips moved back and forth.

Suddenly the headset plugs jerked loose from the recorder and Mrs. McGillicuddy could hear loud music. Mr. McGillicuddy's gyrations became wilder as the music got louder.

The more she watched, the more she laughed, and then she really cackled when the music suddenly stopped and Mr. McGillicuddy continued to shake his hips and rear end. She stood there quietly watching her husband until he finally realized he wasn't hearing any music. When he glanced up after seeing the earplug dangling free, he spotted her. "What are you doing here? You scared the living tar out of me, Jane."

"Oh, don't worry, Mr. Rock and Roll star; you'll be okay." Then she started laughing so hard that tears came to her eyes.

"Oh, stop it," Mr. McGillicuddy whined. "I was just listening to some old rock and roll tapes. I've got to do something to get in the mood to clean this garage."

She kept laughing and stood there pointing at him. "You should have seen yourself."

"Why don't we just forget about the garage and go inside and do some dancing?" he asked with a smile on his face.

But the smile disappeared when she answered, "John, the entertainment was wonderful, but you are not getting out of cleaning the garage. Back the car into the driveway and get to work." And then she turned around and walked to the hallway door and winked at him. "Even great dancers have to work occasionally, John McGillicuddy," she said over her shoulder as she walked back inside the house.

Bobby heard the hallway door to the garage close. He twisted enough to see Mrs. McGillicuddy, with a big grin on her face and laughing, walk into the dining room. She passed through the foyer and down the hallway toward the back bedroom. She mumbled to herself and kept laughing.

When she was out of sight, Bobby leaned over to his Aunt Glaring. *"Are you thinking what I'm thinking, Aunt Glaring?"*

"What am I thinking, Bobby?"

"Mrs. McGillicuddy is getting more and more like Mr. McGillicuddy. She's starting to talk to herself too."

Aunt Glaring laughed. *"That's exactly what I was thinking. But then sometimes I think you are like Mr. McGillicuddy also."*

"What do you mean by that?"

"Well, since the box was moved out of the closet, you've been mumbling to yourself a lot. Are you all right?"

Bobby knew she was correct, but instead of answering her, he asked another question. *"Did you sleep last night, Aunt Glaring?"*

"No, dear. I didn't. That's why I said what I just said. I heard you talking to yourself most of the night. And I heard enough to know you are trying to come up with a plan to get us in the McGillicuddys' luggage so we can go to Spain and be with Remington."

"Yes, but I still haven't figured out how I can do it."

"Oh, you will, dear. I know you will. You always do."

Bobby smiled and hoped she was right. Soon something would happen to help him decide on a plan.

3

Now or Never

Bobby twisted as far as he could inside his pod near the end of the strand. Even lying at the top of the box, he had to lean sideways to see the door. He watched as Mr. McGillicuddy opened it and stepped from the garage into the kitchen hallway. Bobby saw him start to turn and reach back into the garage to get something. And then something happened that made Bobby laugh.

"What are you doing?" Mrs. McGillicuddy asked as she walked through the foyer.

Mr. McGillicuddy nearly fell into the garage. "Oh my gosh! You scared the living daylight out of me. I thought you were in the bedroom bagging up those clothes we're giving away." Mr. McGillicuddy stood, blocking the door-way, and was turned halfway around as he talked over his shoulder.

"I just came up front to get something," she said as she stood staring at her husband. "Would you please tell me why you are standing there with half of your body hanging out the door and the other half twisted like a pretzel?" Mr. McGillicuddy stared back at her, but said nothing.

Mrs. McGillicuddy waited for an answer, but when there was none, she said, "Hello? Hello? Earth to John McGillicuddy. Would you please tell me what is going on?"

"Nothing, dear," he gulped. "Just coming in to get a drink."

"John, do you think I'm a complete dummy?" She walked toward him, and when she did, Mr. McGillicuddy stood up straight and quickly closed the door.

"Are you hiding something?" she asked.

"No, not really."

"What do you mean? You either are hiding something or you are not. Why are you acting so strange?"

"I'm not strange," he whined. "I'm just thirsty. I came in to get something to drink."

"Well, I can understand," she said and laughed. "It's been a whole fifteen minutes since you went out there to work. Why, I bet you feel like you've been in the hot desert all day."

"Oh, quit making fun of me. I really am thirsty."

"Then please"—she smiled—"go get a drink before you dry up and can't work anymore." She laughed again, shook her head, and walked through the foyer and up the stairs to the second floor.

Mr. McGillicuddy walked into the kitchen without another word and reached into the cabinet for a glass. He found a tall one and filled it with ice and water from the automatic dispenser in the refrigerator door. He took a drink and decided to sit down for a moment.

He took his time and enjoyed every sip. When he was finished he said to himself, "I better get that suitcase inside quickly."

But he had waited too long, and he knew it when he heard his wife's voice. "John McGillicuddy, where did this suitcase come from, and who does it belong to?"

"Uh … Uh … Uh, I was just getting ready to tell you."

"Tell me? What were you going to tell me? Where did you find this suitcase? Is this new? The wrapping is still on it. What's going on here?"

"Surprise!" Mr. McGillicuddy said, and he tiptoed up behind his wife and gave her a hug.

"What in the world have you done?"

"It was on sale at Kohl's, and I saw it when I went to buy those house slippers last night. It's my springtime Christmas gift. You needed a new one, and we needed a larger bag to take to Spain for Christmas."

"Oh, John. How sweet of you! Help me pull it inside."

"Just grab the handle and roll it in," he said. "Here, let me tear the plastic off." He reached over and cut a part of the plastic loose with his pocketknife.

She pulled the handle up and rolled the suitcase into the foyer. "This is a huge suitcase," she said. "I'll be able to pack almost everything I need except the clothes I hang in my garment bag."

"What about me?" Mr. McGillicuddy whined. "Do I get to pack anything in there?"

"Well, dear, you have that garment bag I gave you two years ago. And remember, there is a small matching suitcase. Between both of those, you should be fine."

"Well, the most important thing is I wanted you to have this as an early gift for the trip."

"You are wonderful at times, John."

"At times? You mean only at certain times?"

Mrs. McGillicuddy laughed. "Just be happy I think you are wonderful most of the time. Now, get back to work in that garage." She turned and started to roll the suitcase through the foyer, but stopped. "John, I've got an idea."

Mr. McGillicuddy had slowly walked back into the garage. When he heard her, he knew he didn't have to start working yet, so he quickly jumped back into the hallway.

"Let's empty these three old suitcases sitting here in the foyer," she said. "And we'll give them to the women's shelter. There is nothing in there we will ever wear again. We'll give the clothes to the church or another charity. Then we will have plenty of room for my new suitcase. We won't have to pull it up the stairs and put it in the bedroom closet."

Before she could say another word, Mr. McGillicuddy walked into the foyer and dropped down on his knees. He opened the first suitcase and emptied everything onto the floor.

Mrs. McGillicuddy's face broke into a smile as she looked at her new suitcase. "It is very beautiful and makes me want to count the days until we leave for Spain." Then she wheeled it into the closet and placed it against the wall at the end of the line of clothes that were still on the hangers.

Bobby spoke softly to the other bulbs once Mr. and Mrs. McGillicuddy had left the foyer. *"Get ready, we are going back inside for the long wait."*

"Not two years, please. Not that long, Bobby. Can't you get us out for Christmas?"

"I believe I can, Dimmer. I think I finally have a plan that will work. But, let me warn you. You will be in for the toughest eight months of your life. It's going to be difficult.

"I'll explain later. I hear Mr. McGillicuddy coming down the bedroom hall."

Mr. McGillicuddy shoved the box through the doorway. For a moment, he thought he might push it up against the new suitcase near the back of the closet. But he changed his mind, mumbling, "If I do, I'll just have to move it when I get the suitcase out in December. I'll just leave it here at the front."

Bobby waited for one minute just to be sure there was no one outside the door. Then he spoke. *"Good news and bad news, everyone. Mr. McGillicuddy just made it easier for my plan to work."*

"Bobby, you know we are all proud of you," said Dazzling, *"but would you quit being so mysterious? Just tell us and don't make this too dramatic."*

"Oh," he said, *"don't you talk about dramatic. You are the most dramatic of all of us."*

"Bobby, be nice," his mom whispered. *"She's just being Dazzling."*

Bobby nodded and said in a loud voice, *"Here's the good news. Mr. McGillicuddy left the box near the door and the flaps open. This should make it slightly easier, but if my plan works, it is still going to be difficult.*

"As for the bad news, I've still got some planning to do, and the timing has to be right, but one thing is certain, all of us are going to spend about the worst eight months of our life in the darkest place we have ever been. So enjoy the light coming from under the door for the next few days while I wait to get my plan underway."

"You mean it will be darker than all those years at the bottom of the box?" screamed Uncle Glimmer.

"Much darker, I'm afraid," answered Bobby.

"I'm already afraid." It was Dazzling again.

"But it will be worth it," Bobby replied. "If you want something bad enough, then you have to work for it. That's what we will be doing."

Bobby was right. But he didn't realize how difficult things were going to be.

4

The Time for the Plan

For the next two weeks, Bobby and his family spent each day, as they did every year, laying in the box, talking among themselves from time to time, but normally doing nothing. For Bobby it was a time to wait and wonder if what he had overheard the McGillicuddys say would indeed happen. And then, that morning, as the light sneaked under the closet door, he got his answer. The door suddenly flew open and there stood Mr. McGillicuddy.

"I'm getting your blue windbreaker, Jane."

"Good," she said. "Maybe it will bring us luck. Remember, we caught a lot of big fish the last time I wore it." He started to shut the closet door, but Mrs. McGillicuddy stopped him.

"Wait," she said. "Why is the ornament box sitting right in the middle of the doorway? Why don't you slide it to the back of the closet so it is out of the way?"

"But if I do," he answered, "I'll just have to move it back out when we get your suitcase out in December for our trip to Spain."

"Oh, you are something else. It will take five seconds to shove that box to the back of the closet. What's the big deal?"

"I don't know." He smiled and chuckled. "Maybe it would change our fishing luck."

"That did it." She laughed. "Leave it there. Let's go fishing."

Mr. McGillicuddy grinned and closed the door.

Bobby waited until he could no longer hear their footsteps. He wanted to shout out loud and cheer, but he restrained himself.

"What was that all about?" his mom asked.

"I'll tell you in a moment." Then he waited, and within a few seconds, he heard the beeping sound of an alarm as it counted down the time since the door to the garage had been closed. When it finally stopped, he yelled, "Yippee! We just got lucky, and what I overheard Mr. McGillicuddy say is going to happen."

"What's happened?" Dimmer asked.

"Listen up, all of you. If everything works out right, I think I know how to get us to Spain."

The bulbs started cheering, but Bobby shouted, "Give, me a chance to explain. The McGillicuddys have taken what humans call a long weekend. They are driving about two hundred miles to a resort to go fishing. They will be gone today, Saturday, and Sunday, and won't return until the middle of the day on Monday. That means I've got time to make my plan work, but I will need the help of every bulb."

5

The Beginning of the Plan

The McGillicuddys had pulled out of the driveway an hour ago. Mr. McGillicuddy's last words as he walked out of the house were, "Three days of fishing is just what I need after spring-cleaning."

Bobby had once more gone over what the bulbs were going to have to do and the many things he had to do to make sure the plan succeeded. *"We are going to be very lucky if this works,"* said his mom.

"I know," Bobby replied. *"Just keep your filaments crossed that everything goes well."*

"We may need more than filaments crossed if you pull off this plan, Bobby. I hope you have saved up lots of that magical energy."

"Me, too, Mom. I've waited long enough. I don't think the McGillicuddys forgot anything. They aren't returning, so it's time to get to work.

"*Puhrumba! Puhrumba! Puhrumba!*" he roared and twisted as hard as he could. Seconds later, he felt himself begin to unwind from the pod. His plan was underway.

He began to rotate as fast as he ever had before. He felt the power race through his body as he flew toward the ceiling.

There was no question that what he was about to do would require more energy and luck than when he had saved Remington last December; than when he had saved his own dad and cousin Whitening; and it would be an even greater challenge than when he and the bulbs had saved Mrs. McGillicuddy's life last year after the tornado.

"*Whew!*" he said as he hovered beneath the ceiling and looked down at the top of the clothes rack. "*I definitely will need greater powers if I make this happen in this dark closet.*"

"*What's happening, Bobby? I can't see you.*"

He started to answer his mom, but before he could, he heard Aunt Glaring's voice, and then he heard his sister, Sparkle, and cousin Energizer.

"*I can't see you either, nephew.*"

"*Bobby, are you okay?*"

"*I can't see the bulb next to me, let alone you. Let us know what's happening, Bobby.*"

As he hovered, trying to make sure he was in the right spinning mode, Bobby suddenly felt very stupid. He had gained a lot of power and confidence because of some of the heroic things he had done in the past year. However, not once had he ever thought that he might be able to turn a light switch on.

"*What are you doing, son?*"

"Just you watch, Pops."

"How can I watch? I told you I can't see anything," shouted Energizer again.

"You will in a moment." Bobby laughed and slowed down his rotation. He dropped downward in a slow spin and descended below the clothes rack. Then he increased his spinning power and rotated as hard as he could as he moved sideways. When he neared the closet door, he dropped down closer to the floor. From the dim light that crept beneath the door, he was able to see the light switch.

He continued to rotate and managed to move alongside the wall. He was now below the wall plate that covered the switch. "Here I go," he shouted, and he rotated as hard as he could and shrieked, "Puhrumba! Puhrumba! Puhrumba!"

He felt the power as he flew as close as he could to the wall plate. Just as he passed it, he spun even faster and rocked himself back and forth. The surge of air caused the light switch to flip up, and the closet was flooded with light a mini-second later as he rocketed toward the ceiling.

"Oh, my Gosh!" he shouted. He could see everything in the closet. He heard the cheers from below, and he began descending. Better not take any chances, he thought. It was still early in his plan. He continued to slow down his spin, and he was soon hovering over the box. He tilted his head and looked down.

"Way to go, Bobby."

"Unbelievable!"

"You're the bulb, Bobby."

"You're the best."

It was amazing, he thought. All those years in a dark closet and suddenly there was light. As he reduced his spin to the smallest rotation possible, he dropped down into the box and landed on the strand next to Aunt Glaring. She was smiling and so was his mom.

From way beneath him came the deep voice of Uncle Flicker. "Love the light, Bobby, but is there any way you can get us loosened up so we can see more?"

Bobby smiled and spoke loud enough for all the bulbs to hear. "You know, for the first time we have light in the closet, and now we want even more. But I understand. It's just bulb nature."

"What's bulb nature, Bobby?"

"It's just the way we are, Dimmer," he answered his brother. "We always want just a little bit more, no matter how much we have. I think humans are the same way."

With some more magical twists and turns, Bobby went to work to help the other bulbs become more comfortable. He hovered above the top of the box and was able to create a rush of air. Then, he yelled *puhrumba* three times. The current he created began to pull the strand into the air.

"We're flying. We're flying," bellowed Uncle Flicker.

"This is unreal," shouted his cousin Energizer.

Even shy little Blushing had something to say. *"Bobby, this is fun. Can you keep us hanging here in the air for a while?"*

But Bobby could already feel his powers weakening. He reduced the flow of the air current and dropped the strand back onto the top of the other strands, giving all of the Bright family a better view.

"This is fantastic, Bobby. Thank you."

"My pleasure, Aunt Shining," and as he said it, Bobby bowed forward in mid-flight, as if he were an entertainer waiting for applause.

And that is exactly what he got. The bulbs clapped their filaments and cheered once more. It made him feel good, and he knew it would help him, because the hard work was still ahead. He settled himself back down by the strand. A short rest was needed before he could summon his powers again.

"Explain it to me one more time, Bobby," Aunt Glaring said. He was sitting next to her, but outside his pod. There was no need to screw himself back in. He was just getting started.

"Okay, here's the plan. I could never do this with the McGillicuddys in the house because it would be too noisy. First, I have to get the suitcase to tip over and land upright. I don't think that will be too tough," he explained. *"Then, I will have to get the main part of the suitcase unzipped. That will be real difficult."*

"Why the main part, Bobby? I know you want to hide us in the suitcase, but if we were in one of those small side pockets, wouldn't it be easier to unzip than the big zipper?"

"You're right, it would be, but it would be too easy for Mrs. McGillicuddy to see us when she starts packing. I hope when I get the suitcase opened there will be some pockets inside that will be large enough to hide in."

And it wasn't long until Bobby got his wish.

The suitcase lay on the floor. It had been easier than Bobby thought it would be. After a brief rest, he had produced more energy. Then he had once again spun as fast as he could and flown to the ceiling. Once there, he had nosedived down to the suitcase. When he neared it, he made a move that looked like a reverse high dive and swept right in front of it.

The draft of air created by the movement caused the suitcase to rock back and forth. It almost fell forward, but remained standing. He completed a swooping arc, and as he neared the ceiling again, he turned and looked down. He saw it rocking back and forth. He had a chance, if he hurried, to complete the first part of his plan before the suitcase quit shaking.

He rushed downward and flew by the front of the suit-case, twisting back and forth as he passed it. The rush of air was just enough to force the piece of luggage to tilt forward, and it fell to the floor. *Kerplunk!*

"*What's that noise?*" shouted Bingo.

"*Bobby just made the suitcase fall over. It just hit the floor,*" answered Energizer.

The bulbs started cheering, but Bobby admonished, "Don't get too excited yet. The hardest part is still ahead."

6
Completing the Plan

This was tougher than Bobby had imagined. He wasn't sure how many times he had tried to fly around the sides of the fallen suitcase. He knew at least a couple of hours had passed while he tried and tried, with no success, to make the zipper start moving around its track so he could open the main part of the suitcase.

He had lost most of his power. He flew back to the top of the box and dropped down into his pod. He was so tired; he didn't even twist himself the few turns it would have taken to fit snugly inside. He just leaned sideways against his mom and fell asleep.

After taking a nap, Bobby woke up and was surprised as he looked up at the light fixture on the ceiling of the closet. It was the first time he had ever awakened to a lighted closet. It felt weird.

"*Did you have a good nap, Bobby?*" his mom asked. When he didn't answer, she asked, "*Well, did you?*"

"Did I? Did I what?"

"I just asked you if you had a good nap."

"Oh, yeah. Sure. Yes. Yeah! I think."

"Are you alright, Bobby?" Aunt Glaring leaned over from the other side and stared at him.

"Uh, sure. I'm okay, Aunt Glaring." Then he looked at his mom. "I'm okay, Mom. It's just that I woke up and couldn't believe how light it is."

"We know," said Aunt Glaring sternly. "We've been trying to go to sleep but it's too bright in here. No one wanted to wake you up. Now, please turn off the light. I'm sure it is nighttime."

She started to say something else but Dazzling interrupted. "It would be very nice if you did so, Bobby. The glare is just too much. It is awful."

"All right," he said. "I'm sure you need your beauty rest." Dimmer, Bingo, and Energizer all began to laugh.

"There's nothing funny about this, Robert. I need my sleep."

"Of course you do, Miss Beauty Queen."

"Bobby, that's enough," his mom whispered. "Be nice. You know she is different."

"Okay, Dazzling. My mom, the real queen, has granted you your wish."

Bobby quickly rotated himself into motion and flew out of the box. Once he reached the ceiling, he immediately swooped downward. Bobby increased his speed, and as he flew past the wall switch, the air current from his bottom produced so much pressure that the switch flicked to the off position. The closet became pitch dark. The bulbs cheered, and the sound of filaments clapping filled the small space.

When the applause stopped, the bulbs waited for Bobby to say something. But there was no sound. "Are you all right?" Bobby's dad asked.

"I don't hear him," said Bobby's mom.

"Bobby. Bobby, where are you?" yelled Sparkle.

There was no answer, just the quiet sound of crying, or was that laughter?

"Bobby? Is that you?" Aunt Glaring meant business when she sounded like this. "You answer me, and don't tease your family. Are you okay?" Bobby started laughing.

Uncle Flicker's voice crashed through the darkness. "Bobby Bright. Stop that laughing and tell us if you are okay. Tell us right now." The laughing stopped, but there was no answer. "Do you hear me, Bobby?" yelled Uncle Flicker.

After a few more seconds Bobby said, "Sorry, everyone. That was wild, scary, and fun, all at the same time."

"What happened, brother?"

"When I flashed past the light switch and the room turned dark, I tried to turn and arch my body so I could drift down into the box. But I lost power and flew straight on to the top of the suitcase. I was lucky. I could have crashed into the wall."

"Oh my gosh, my baby. Are you hurt?"

"No. I'm lucky, Mom. But I'll have to be careful whenever I turn the light off. Don't worry. I'm okay. I'm going to go to sleep here."

When Bobby awoke, there was light shining from the foyer beneath the door. He looked around and spotted something opposite of where he was lying. He whispered two quick *Puhrumbas* and rolled toward the other side. What he saw made him smile. He yelled *puhrumba* three more times and flew toward the darkened ceiling. Then he dropped downward and sped by the light switch, producing enough power to make it flip on. Light flooded the room.

"*Were you going to sleep all day?*" Twinkle shouted from below.

Bobby drifted downward into the box. "*What do you mean?*"

"*Well, I have no idea how to tell time or to keep track of it, but I do know that everyone in your family has been awake for a long time. We've been whispering among ourselves because we didn't want to wake you up.*"

"*I must have really worn myself out last night.*"

"*Yes, you did,*" she answered. "*And I hope everything you are doing is going to be worth it.*"

"Funny you said that, Mom, because I have finally discovered how we are going to get to Spain in that suitcase, and it's time for me to get back to work.

"Puhrumba! Puhrumba! Puhrumba!"

Bobby's magical powers produced quite a show that day. It was fun to watch. Most of the bulbs had a great view, and the ones that couldn't see quite as well still got to hear Bobby's brother. Dimmer had always been kind of shy and quiet, but not today. He became like one of those play-by-play announcers on a sports broadcast. He chattered away in *Bulbese,* explaining everything that his brother was doing through the exciting Saturday afternoon.

Bobby lay on top of the suitcase, exhausted from his day's work. But it had certainly been worth it. He was inside the suitcase. It wasn't the main part, but a smaller storage space on the outside of the suitcase near the top. He had spotted it when he had awakened earlier in the day. It was a place for small items, like socks and underwear and maybe even small gifts the McGillicuddys might bring for Remington and his parents.

Most important, thought Bobby, *it will be our hiding place.*

It had taken the rest of the day to get the zipper around the track so the flap would come open. It had taken six more attempts to pull the flap into the air and get it to fall back to the side of the suitcase.

"Are you resting, Bobby?"

40

"Yes, Mom. You guys have chattered all day. If you are ready to stop, I'm ready to go to sleep."

"We'll be quiet. It's just that we have been so excited. It was like watching some kind of a show. Maybe like one of those television shows that humans watch. Remember when we used to be stuck at the back of the big tree and you would tell us the McGillicuddys were watching television?"

"Yeah, I remember. Does that mean I'm a TV star?"

"Well, I don't know about that." Aunt Glaring giggled. "But it sure means you have entertained us. Don't bother with the light. We'll sleep with it on tonight. You have to be ready for tomorrow, although I don't know how you are going to make all this happen."

"Don't worry," Bobby answered, "It will happen."

And it did, although it wasn't easy.

There was only one full day left to get the rest of the plan completed. It was Sunday morning. Some of the other bulbs were still sleeping when Bobby awoke and went back to work.

"Puhrumba! Puhrumba! Puhrumba! Puhrumba!" He put an extra one in for good measure, so he could generate as much energy as possible. He had awakened many times during the night, each time worrying about whether he could actually transfer the strand from the box to the suitcase. It was going to be a challenge, and he would need plenty of strength.

He spun into the air and lifted away from the top of the suitcase. *"All of you, wake up,"* he shouted as he gained the necessary rotation speed. He flew up above the clothes rack.

"What are you doing, Bobby?"

"Good morning, Energizer," he said as he turned and headed back down toward the open top of the box. Then, as he neared it, he put the brakes on and swooped back toward the ceiling again. As he approached, he turned right and then left, as if he were practicing different techniques.

"Wow!" Energizer yelled from below. *"Why are you putting on a show, Bobby?"*

"Just warming up. Is everyone awake down there?"

"I think so." Energizer looked at the bulbs nearest him in the middle of the strand and screamed, *"Is everyone awake?"*

Aunt Glaring shouted back, *"Well, Energizer, should we wait for the bulbs that are asleep to tell us they are awake?"* Most of the bulbs started laughing.

Blinker yelled from the far end, *"I'm still asleep, Energizer."*

Then there was more laughter. *"All right,"* Energizer shouted back. *"I get the point."*

"What's going on down there?" asked Bobby as he reduced his rotation and drifted down close to the bulbs.

"*We are all awake,*" said Energizer. "*Now, tell us what's going to happen.*"

When Bobby had finished explaining how he planned to get the entire strand transferred to the suitcase and placed inside the pocket, he said, "*This is going to be the most exciting and dangerous thing we have ever done.*"

"*Even more dangerous than when you lifted your Aunt Shining, Blinker, and me off the floor and pushed us into the wall socket?*" asked Uncle Flicker.

Bobby recalled the moment last spring when the bulbs had saved Mrs. McGillicuddy after she had been injured during the tornado. In order to do so, the plug on the strand had to be plugged into the wall socket. He was able to create enough airflow while spinning in the air to lift the plug off the ground and jam it into the socket. Since Uncle Flicker, Aunt Shining, and Blinker lived closest to the plug, they were the ones actually pulled into the air.

"*This is going to be much scarier and wilder.*"

And it was.

"*You are unbelievable, Bobby,*" shouted Uncle Flicker. He was right beneath Bobby, looking up at him. Flicker really didn't understand how his nephew had done it, but he had.

Bobby had rotated the base of his body in between the two covered wires of the strand. Then he had twisted the top of his body and managed to get the electrical plug to loop around his neck.

"We're in the air again and flying, Shining. Just like last year."

"Oh, I know, Flicker. I know we are flying." Bobby heard more than just Aunt Shining screaming. He heard all kinds of shouts from below. *Thank goodness,* he thought, *the ceiling is only ten feet high.* He had lifted the strand high enough out of the box so none of the bulbs would hit the floor as he crossed toward the suitcase.

He was very worried about the broken top of his dad's head and whether he would be okay during the trip, but there was nothing he could do now except hope.

"Quiet!" He yelled as loud as he could. *"Quiet! Calm down, everyone."*

Bobby was already starting to get weak. Halfway from the box to the suitcase, he was having trouble rotating as fast as he needed to in order to keep the nearly seven-foot-long strand from dropping to the floor. He thought of his, dad, mom, and Aunt Glaring at the opposite end. They would be the first to hit the floor if he lost power.

Even though it was only five feet from the box to the suitcase, a short distance by human standards, it was a journey for a magical bulb with his entire family hanging beneath him. He was getting weaker by the second, but he became excited when he looked down and saw the strand nearly above the suitcase. They had almost made it when he heard shouts that meant trouble.

"*I just hit the side of the suitcase,*" screamed Aunt Glaring.

"*Me too,*" shrieked Bobby's mom.

"Bobby," Aunt Glaring yelled, "*I'm hitting the side of the suitcase. So are your mom and dad.*"

He and the strand began to drop downward.

This time, he recognized his mom's voice. "*We are about to hit the floor.*"

Aunt Glaring screamed, "*I just did. I bounced off of it. That hurt.*"

Bobby knew his mom and dad would be next. If his dad hit the floor, the rest of the already broken top of his head might smash into tiny pieces. He was filled with fear until he looked back down and saw the face of his toughest cousin, Energizer. He was the only bulb in his family that Bobby believed was as tough as he was. When he saw the scowl on Energizer's face and the look of disbelief that Bobby was going to fail, it was all he needed.

He felt brave again and shouted louder than ever before, "*Puhrumba! Puhrumba! Puhrumba!*" With one super bulb effort, he spun the strand around and around and sailed almost to the top of the ceiling. Now, he knew for sure he was high enough, and he shifted a foot to his right and peered down. The whole strand was above the middle of the open flap on the suitcase.

"*Zerplonk,*" he screamed, and the strand started to fall into the suitcase. He could only imagine what it was like at the other end.

"*Oh, that feels good,*" shouted Aunt Glaring. She had just touched the inside of the suitcase.

"*Ouch! I just bumped into you. Sorry, Glaring,*" Bobby's mom said.

Bobby's dad gently rolled off the side of his wife and nestled up against her.

As Bobby descended toward the suitcase, he heard lots of apologies and bulbs saying they were sorry as they clanked against each other. But most importantly, they were all happy. The whole strand was in the suitcase. A few moments later, they all applauded. Bobby Bright, their hero, had settled in beside them. Near one end of the strand, he lay still and exhausted but with a smile on his face.

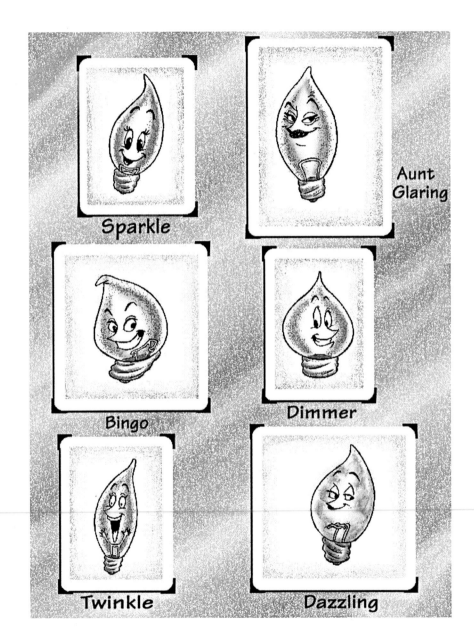

PART TWO

7

Arrival in Madrid

Except for a trip to Canada many years ago to visit a relative they had only seen one other time in their life, the McGillicuddys had never been out of the United States. That all changed on the morning of December 17. After changing planes in Chicago, they flew directly to Madrid. The flight took eight and one half hours, but it was over ten hours before they actually landed at Barajas Airport. A foggy morning kept the plane circling in a holding pattern until finally the captain announced to the passengers there was enough visibility to land.

"Look, John," Mrs. McGillicuddy said as she stared out the window. "I can see the city. Oh my gosh, I've never seen so many apartment buildings in my life."

Mr. McGillicuddy leaned across his wife and peered through the window. "Wow! You're right. Are there any houses down there or only apartments?" As far as he could see, there were tall apartment buildings intermingled with a few other skyscrapers.

The voice of one of the stewards on the plane came over the loud speaker. *"Por favor, siéntese ahorita.* Please

sit down," he immediately added in English. "We are landing within seconds."

"Some goofball just stood up to get something out of
the luggage bin. Don't people know to sit down when they
are landing?"

Mrs. McGillicuddy smiled and started laughing. "Oh,
John," she said. "You're suddenly the big time, experienced flyer."

Before he could argue, the wheels of the Iberia 747
touched down on Spanish land. Fifteen minutes after
landing, the McGillicuddy's finally left the plane. After
walking through the jet way, they entered a hall and
were met by airline employees speaking both English and
Spanish and giving directions. For five minutes they followed the crowd, and then, as they started to step onto
an escalator to go down to the baggage area, they were
able to see giant carousels with luggage circling round
and round.

"Somewhere down there is our luggage," said Mrs.
McGillicuddy, "I only hope we can find all of it."

The McGillicuddy's soon learned that nothing went
swiftly, and by the time they had gone through customs,
had their passports checked, found their luggage, had it
inspected, and finally left the foreign travelers arrival
area, nearly thirty minutes had passed.

When they finally reached the outer door, they were looking into the faces of about fifty Spaniards still waiting for friends and relatives.

Mr. McGillicuddy first noticed six or seven car rental counters behind the crowd of greeters. He could also see some other airport stores and a sign that read "*Restaurante*" and a booth with a sign above that said "*Información.*"

"Do you see them, John? Richard told me they would be waiting outside the baggage and customs area."

At that moment the McGillicuddys reached the end of the roped off area and followed the passengers in front of them into the main terminal. Suddenly a man with a dirty beard and old, tattered clothes jumped in front of Mrs. McGillicuddy.

"What are you doing?" yelled Mr. McGillicuddy.

"*Ayudame. Dinero, por favor.*"

"Get away from her," yelled a woman from the group of people standing to the side.

Mr. McGillicuddy stepped forward, and the man backed away from Mrs. McGillicuddy and shuffled away into the crowd.

"That's Lisa's voice, John. There she is. In fact, there they all are," she screamed, and raced forward into the crowd, leaving Mr. McGillicuddy pushing the cart filled with luggage. He spotted Remington for the first time.

The little redhead jumped into his grandmother's arms. Mr. McGillicuddy watched for a few seconds and then said, "It's my turn to get some sugar," and he reached down and picked up his grandson and gave him a huge hug.

"Did that stinking old dirty beggar touch you or grandma?"

"No. But what did he want?"

"He was just asking for money, Grandpa. Those homeless people are gross. They are always begging for money or *dinero,* as they say."

"Remington, don't be ugly," said his mom.

"Everything okay?" asked Remington's dad as he joined the group.

"We're fine. We're fine," proclaimed Mrs. McGillicuddy, who reached up and hugged her son. "Don't worry about that. We are so happy just to be here safely."

"Well, welcome to Madrid, Grandma and Grandpa."

Then the five of them each took turns hugging each other.

Just a few feet away, inside Mrs. McGillicuddy's new suitcase, there was also excitement.

Inside the top zippered flap, hidden among silk stockings, scarves, underwear, and even a couple of caps, were Bobby Bright and his family of bulbs. The trip for them had been very, very difficult, but Bobby shouted to all of his family scrunched together and hidden in the darkness, "I just heard Remington's voice."

As tired and miserable as they were from first being hidden in the suitcase for over seven months and then for the past two days, covered with clothes, it all seemed worth it. They knew it wouldn't be long until the suitcase would open, and they would be discovered. And when they were, they knew Remington would be the happiest boy in Spain.

8

Look What's in the Suitcase

Mrs. McGillicuddy opened her suitcase and looked around the guest bedroom in the apartment. "This is larger than I expected," she said. "It's very nice, and those bullfighting prints on the wall are very exciting. They almost look like actual photographs."

Mr. McGillicuddy didn't respond. He stood at the window, looking down onto a very narrow street, only large enough for one small car to travel between the curbs. When his eyes drifted upward, he saw nearly a dozen television antennas, each one a different size and shape and each one standing between curved pieces of clay-colored tile that covered the roof of the building across the street.

"John, open your suitcase and unpack. We're not going to leave the clothes in the luggage for three weeks."

He started to say something but was interrupted by her scream. "Oh my gosh! There's a snake or something in my suitcase." She slammed the top down and backed away from the bag, which was sitting on the bed.

"What are you talking about?"

"I'm serious. Look inside." She stood staring at her suitcase.

"Do I need to get a rake or a shovel from Richard so I can hit it?"

"Real funny," she said. "Just open it."

Mr. McGillicuddy tiptoed across the room, acting like he was afraid to approach the bag. Then he suddenly threw it open and went, "Eeeek." Then he laughed loudly.

"Oh, you are really funny. Just tell me; is there something in there?"

He removed a small bag of books and one of her sweaters and placed them on the bedspread. "I don't see any animals, Jane." He reached back in the suitcase and pulled out a small robe.

"Well, something moved," she insisted. "It looked green."

"I don't see anything," he answered.

"Well, you're not looking in the right part," she said. "It's under the upper flap where my scarves and your caps are."

He reached back in the suitcase and pulled out a baseball cap, and then it was his turn to scream. "Oh my goodness. Will you look at this?" he said. "You're right; there is something in here, and I can't believe it."

"Is it green? Is it long? Is it moving?"

Mr. McGillicuddy chuckled and said, "Yes, yes, no." He waited for a reply, but his wife just scowled at him with her hands on her hips.

"That's my answer to each of your questions," he said.

"What do you mean?"

"Yes, it is green; yes, it is long; and no, it is not moving."

"What is it, please?"

"Jane, you know very well what it is. You put it there, and I think it's a fabulous idea. How did you know it was the right strand?"

"What are you talking about?"

He reached inside and pulled out the strand of bulbs. "Voila! Just like magic, my dear. The Christmas tree lights are with us. A brilliant idea to bring them, and we can put them on Remington's tree."

She stood like a statue, gazing at Mr. McGillicuddy, who was holding part of the strand in his hands while the rest dangled downward toward the floor. "How did those bulbs get in the suitcase?" She waited for his answer, but Mr. McGillicuddy said nothing. The two just stood there looking at each other.

Finally, when she didn't speak, he said, "Jane, you did put them there, right?"

She shook her head. "No, I did not, and you know I didn't, John. You pulled one of your tricks, didn't you?"

"My dear, I didn't put those bulbs in the suitcase."

It seemed longer, but it was really only ten seconds that the two stood staring at each other.

"You are making me laugh," Mrs. McGillicuddy said. "You should see yourself, standing there with your mouth wide open."

"Well, you are making me laugh, too. Your mouth is as wide open as mine." Mrs. McGillicuddy started to answer, but he continued. "You see, my dear, you caught me before I could surprise you."

"John McGillicuddy, what are you saying? Did you put these bulbs in the suitcase and not tell me?"

Mr. McGillicuddy didn't get a chance to answer, and he was glad he didn't. He certainly didn't want to lie, but he certainly didn't want to believe what he was thinking.

The voice of Remington's mom saved the day. "Are you two arguing in there?" she shouted from outside the bedroom door.

Just as she started to knock, the door was pulled open, and she stumbled forward through the doorway, right into the arms of Mr. McGillicuddy. "Is my daughter-in-law so happy to see me she's fallen into my arms?"

She laughed and asked, "What's going on in here?"

Mrs. McGillicuddy started explaining about the bulbs. When she told her daughter-in-law she had first believed there was a snake in the suitcase, all three of them laughed.

"Well, when you get finished unpacking, come on downstairs. I have some great pastries from one of our favorite shops here in Madrid. You both are going to love all the different rolls and muffins and creamy *tortas* they make here in Spain."

"Don't go, Lisa. We'll walk downstairs with you to the kitchen. Let me hang up a couple of these dresses in the closet."

Meanwhile, Mr. McGillicuddy had sauntered over to one of the windows overlooking the balcony. He looked down at the very narrow one-lane street below. There were couples and groups of three and four persons walking along the sidewalk. Whenever a car would approach from the top of the hill, those people on the sidewalk would quickly get in a straight line and walk single file. It was necessary to protect yourself from accidentally being hit by an auto as it passed.

Even though he was staring out the window, his real thoughts were on that strand of bulbs. He continued to ponder how they could have gotten in the suitcase. He knew he hadn't placed them there. But the longer he stood there, the more he tried to convince himself that maybe he had.

He was almost certain it was the same strand that the McGillicuddys had named "miracle bulbs" after it was determined they had helped save Mrs. McGillicuddy's life after the tornado had hit the McGillicuddy's home last year. He believed the bulbs had helped stop the bleeding on her badly cut leg.

"Are you deaf, John McGillicuddy?"

"What, dear?" He turned around to look at her, but when he did, he shuddered for a second and a cold chill ran down his spine. His eyes caught sight of the real dark blue bulb near the end of the strand. It was the one Remington claimed was named Bobby.

"Is there something wrong with you, Dad?"

Mr. McGillicuddy just stood there staring into the suitcase.

"John, answer Lisa."

"Sorry, ladies. I was just daydreaming."

"That's not a surprise. You are always daydreaming," Mrs. McGillicuddy said, and then the two women started laughing as they walked out of the room and into the hallway.

He wandered back to the balcony door and peered through the glass. "How did they get inside the suitcase?" he mumbled to himself. "We certainly didn't put them there."

He didn't have an answer for the mystery, but he would agree with whatever his wife wanted to believe, and to make things easier, he would take credit for bringing the bulbs to Spain.

9

First, a Christmas Tree

Remington burst through the bedroom doorway, jumped into his grandfather's arms, and gave him a big hug.

"You've gotten bigger, young man, since you turned nine years old."

"Do you think so, Grandpa?"

"Yes I do," and he stood his grandson back down on the floor.

Remington backed away and looked up at Mr. McGillicuddy with a quizzical look on his face. "You know what, Grandpa? I just thought of something. Where is Rocket? Didn't he get to come to Spain?"

Mr. McGillicuddy laughed, and said, "Rocket's not here. He's back in the states."

Remington paused for a moment, and then frowned as he looked at Mr. McGillicuddy. "You mean you left him in the doghouse for the whole time you're in Spain!"

Mr. McGillicuddy grinned and shook his head. "No, sport. We left him at a dog kennel where he'll be fed and watered daily by the people who take care of pets for a living. He has lots of other dogs to run around with while he is there, and your grandma left him so many Christmas biscuits that he will definitely need the exercise."

Remington's face relaxed into a smile, and Mr. McGillicuddy reached out his hand to playfully scruff his hair. "Has your hair gotten redder, Remington?"

The grin vanished.

"No, Grandpa, and I don't have time to talk about that right now anyway. This is serious."

"What is it?" Mr. McGillicuddy asked.

"It's time to go get the Christmas tree."

"You mean you don't have a tree yet?" Mrs. McGillicuddy asked as she stepped back in from the hallway.

"No," squealed Remington. "We waited for you to get here."

"But it's just one week until Christmas."

"Oh, Grandma, you've got a lot to learn. You are in Spain. We've got lots of time."

"What's he talking about, Lisa?"

Remington spoke before his mom could answer. "Just you wait and see, Grandma, and you too, Grandpa. I'll explain later. Right now, it's time to go get our Christmas trees at the *Plaza Mayor.*"

"What is the—?" Mrs. McGillicuddy stopped in midsentence. "Uuuh... the Plaza?"

Remington finished the sentence as he walked over to her and gave her a hug. "*Mayor,* Grandma," he said. "It is pronounced, My-or. It is the most famous plaza in all of Spain."

Mrs. McGillicuddy started to ask where it was but never got the question out of her mouth. Remington screamed loudly, "Oh my gosh! You brought my buddies." He turned and jumped into his grandmother's arms.

"Whoa!" she said. "You are getting too heavy for me, Mr. Nine-year-old."

Remington's dad came racing into the room. "Are you all right, Remington?"

Remington didn't answer. He was too excited. "You did it!" Remington said and slid back out of Mrs. McGillicuddy's arms. "You brought Bobby and his family. You brought my buddies to Spain. Look, Mom. Look, Dad." He pointed at the bulbs in the suitcase. "They're the same bulbs that have been on my tree the last two years. Grandma, Grandpa, you are so smart. This is the best Christmas present I could ever have gotten."

Mrs. McGillicuddy said, "This is all your grandpa's doing. I don't know why he brought the bulbs, but if you are happy, then I'm glad they are here."

"Thank you so much, Grandpa." Remington ran and jumped into Mr. McGillicuddy's arms.

He hugged his grandson tightly then let him slide out of his arms, and the two of them walked to the window. Maybe just he and Remington would have to have their own special talk about this later, but he did know for sure that from this moment on, everyone would always believe he had put the bulbs in the suitcase. It would be his secret forever.

It took Mr. and Mrs. McGillicuddy twenty minutes to unpack their clothes and get settled into their bedroom. Remington was anxious to go shopping for the Christmas trees and ran into the room three times to ask them if they were ready to go. Finally, they were, and everyone gathered at the front door of the apartment.

"All right. Are we ready?" Remington's dad asked.

"I've been ready for twenty minutes, Daddy," Remington squealed. "So let's get going."

"Is that coat going to be warm enough for you?" Remington's mom asked Mrs. McGillicuddy.

"Yes, this jacket is a lot warmer than it looks."

"Are you okay, Grandpa? It's cold here in Madrid, but not as cold as back home." He paused for a moment, and when there was no answer, he said, "Then let's go."

Everyone laughed as they walked out the front door and headed for the nearby elevator. As Remington's dad started to lock the door, Remington suddenly yelled, "Wait, I forgot something." He raced past his father and back into the apartment.

"Hurry," his mom yelled. "The elevator is almost here."

Bobby and the bulbs were lying in a twisted heap next to a large brown and orange cushion. Mrs. McGillicuddy had removed the strand from the suitcase and placed them on a small love seat that sat in the corner of the bedroom. When Mr. McGillicuddy had changed into a clean shirt, he had tossed the one worn on the plane onto the couch. It covered part of the bulbs.

Bobby heard Remington before he saw him dash through the bedroom doorway. "I'm coming to get you," Remington whispered.

From underneath the shirt, Bobby saw Remington run to the suitcase sitting on the foot of the bed. He looked inside but apparently didn't find what he wanted. And then, a moment later, Remington picked up the shirt and squealed, "There you are, you wonderful bulbs."

Bobby heard the voice of Remington's dad in the distance. "Get down here right now, Remington McGillicuddy."

Remington's hand grabbed the strand and fumbled with it. "There you are, my wonderful, dark blue friend. It's you; I know it's you, Bobby." Bobby felt Remington's fingers grab a hold of him. He wondered what was going to happen, and then he found out as Remington started unscrewing Bobby.

"*What's he doing?*" Bobby's mom whispered. "*Where's he taking you?*"

"*I'll be okay, Mom.*" Bobby didn't have time to say anything else.

"Remington McGillicuddy, what are you doing in here? I finally sent your grandparents down to the lobby. Daddy is still waiting at the elevator."

He turned and stuck his hand in his pocket. He could feel the blue bulb. "Nothing, Mom. I just wanted to tell the bulbs they would be hanging on a Christmas tree before the day was over." He tried to give her his best smile possible.

"And you ran back in here to tell them that?" she said sarcastically.

"Mom, it's okay. I'm not weird like you think I am."

"I don't think you are weird, but you are weird when it comes to these bulbs."

"Okay," Remington whined, "Maybe a little weird, but it's just fun to have them here so I can put them on the tree."

And then, Remington rushed from the room, yelling over his shoulder, "Let's go, so we can get our trees!"

Deep in the pocket of Remington's pants, Bobby chuckled at what he had heard. Then, he felt the fingers wrap around him, and he was pulled from the pocket. He could see a narrow hall and a mirror on the wall. He was actually looking at himself in the hands of Remington, who said, "I'm going to show you some neat things in Madrid, Bobby, but we've got to be careful."

And then Bobby felt the tiny hand close around him and back he went into the pocket.

Once everyone reached the narrow street in front of the apartment, Remington let his parents and grandparents get in front of him on the narrow sidewalk. He reached into his pocket and pulled out the bulb. "Listen, Bobby. I will try and keep you outside my pocket to show you some different things, but I won't be able to all of the time." Then he tucked the bulb back inside his pocket and raced down the sidewalk to catch up with his grandpa.

"Next stop, *Plaza Mayor*," Remington said as he grabbed a hold of Mr. McGillicuddy's hand.

They walked up the majestic *Gran Via,* with department stores, fancy restaurants, and giant theatres featuring Broadway-type musicals. It took a long time because Mrs. McGillicuddy wanted to stop and look at the leather purses and suitcases and stylish dresses that were in the store windows.

"Do you think we could go inside this women's shop for just a quick look?" Mrs. McGillicuddy asked her daughter-in-law. "Richard, John, and Remington appear to be buying something from that street vendor."

"Sure. Let's sneak in and take a peek at the dresses that are too expensive for us." But they never got the chance.

Almost a half a block away, Remington's dad handed his son a sack of fresh chestnuts that had just been scooped from a huge hot pan filled with sizzling hot coals. Suddenly they heard a scream.

"What's happening?" asked Mr. McGillicuddy. "That sounds like Jane's voice."

They all turned their heads to look down the street and saw Mrs. McGillicuddy. Behind her, Remington's mom yelled, "He's chasing us."

Both women were nearly running, and behind them, hobbling on one crutch and trying to catch them was a tall man in a long tattered overcoat. He held a dirty cap upside down in his left hand. As he shook it, coins rattled inside, and he was yelling, *"Por favor. Por favor."*

Suddenly Remington ran away from his dad and grandfather and raced toward his grandmother. *"Vaya, Vaya,"* he screamed at the man, just as he felt the hand of his dad on his shoulder. "Stop, Remington. I'll take care of it," and he stepped forward and held his hand up. *"Alto! Dejanos, ahorita!"*

The man nearly fell as he stopped. Then he mumbled something in Spanish and turned to slowly shuffle away.

"He grabbed my coat as we started to go into one of those shops, and he was begging for money," said Mrs. McGillicuddy. "I did recognize the word, *dinero.*"

"I told him to go away, Grandma," Remington said proudly. "Why does he have to bother people?"

"Well," Mrs. McGillicuddy huffed, "he should get a job. I don't like those bums."

"Mom! Remington! Both of you watch what you say. There may be a reason he can't work. He is handicapped," said Richard. "You and I will talk more about this later."

"Yes, Daddy," Remington whined.

"Now let's forget this," said his dad, "and let's get the *Plaza Mayor.*"

After a slow stroll along the pedestrian avenue, *Calle de Preciados,* to the world famous *Puerta del Sol,* it had been more than forty-five minutes since they had left the apartment.

Working their way through the late afternoon crowd of workers and shoppers and tourists, they finally approached the steps to one of the more than half a dozen entrances to the *Plaza Mayor.* Remington ran around the four adults and standing on the bottom step, dramatically said, *"Permítame a introducirles a la Plaza Mayor."*

"Oh my goodness," gushed Mrs. McGillicuddy. "John, we have our very own guide."

Mr. McGillicuddy laughed. "Yes, we do. But we don't understand Spanish. I wonder if he speaks English."

"Yes, I do, sir," Remington said with a great big smile on his face. "But you tell them, Dad. Tell them what I said."

"Remington is getting very good with his basic Spanish," Richard answered. "He just told you, 'Allow me to introduce you to the *Plaza Mayor*.'"

It had been dark for over an hour. The temperature was in the mid thirties, and even though there were hundreds and hundreds of people shopping at the rows and rows of Christmas booths in the middle of the plaza, there wasn't enough body heat to stay warm.

"I'm pretty chilly," Mrs. McGillicuddy said. "But this is so exciting; I don't even mind it. These buildings are so beautiful with their unique architecture. And those murals are amazing. It was very pretty in the daylight, but this is absolutely beautiful with all of the lights shining on these buildings.

"Are these all apartments?" she asked her daughter-in-law.

"Most of them," Lisa answered, "but that one over there"—she pointed to the far corner of the square—"is the *Casa de la Panadería*. It was built at the end of the sixteenth century, even before the square was designed."

Remington held the blue bulb up in front of his face. "See, Bobby, you can learn from my mom too. I don't have to talk all of the time." Then he chuckled. "Even though I have been."

Suddenly, Remington's mom turned, and he was just able to stick his hand in his right pocket and drop the bulb to the bottom. "What are you doing, Remington?"

"Nothing, Mom. Just waiting for Dad and Grandpa to get back with the hot chocolate and the popcorn."

"Well, I wish they would hurry. I'm ready to find our two Christmas trees."

"Me too."

"Where are the taller trees, Remington?" Mrs. McGillicuddy asked. "All I've seen have been these small bare ones. They don't have many branches."

"I'm afraid that's what we are going to get, Grandma. They won't be like the huge tree you and Grandpa always have downstairs at your house. They are more like the tiny one you got for me the last two years. They will be perfect for Bobby and the other bulbs you brought me."

"Well, he's right about that," Remington's mom said to Mrs. McGillicuddy. "They are small. It's funny, though, how Remington's idea of a Christmas tree has changed. When he was in kindergarten and the first grade, he used to go back to school after we would visit you for Christmas, and he would brag to all his friends that his grandparents had the biggest Christmas tree in the world." His mom turned to Remington. "You have to admit you didn't say anything about those tall trees the last two years. All you talked about at school was your own tree in the guest room and, of course, about those magical bulbs of yours."

Remington wrapped his hand around the bulb in his pocket and gave it a squeeze. "Yep," Remington said. "I've loved my trees at your house the last two years, Grandma."

"We're back," Remington's dad said as he walked up behind him.

"Eeeek! You scared me, Daddy. Where's Grandpa?" He stepped around his dad, who held a cardboard tray of cups filled with hot chocolate in one hand and a huge bag of popcorn in the other. All he saw were hundreds of people shopping for ornaments, bulbs, and other Christmas decorations throughout the plaza.

"Where is he, Dad?" Remington said over his shoulder as he watched people passing by. "Do you see him anywhere?"

"How about you turn around and look directly behind you?" And when Remington did, there was Mr. McGillicuddy acting like a nine-year-old himself. He jumped out from behind one of the booths and hollered, "Look what I've got."

In his left hand was a long, long rope, and on it, evenly spaced, were three different Santa Clauses appearing to be climbing the rope. An identical rope with the same number of Santa Claus figures was also in his right hand.

"Wow!" Remington exclaimed. "How did you know I wanted these, Grandpa?"

"A Spanish bird told me," Mr. McGillicuddy said and laughed.

"You told him, didn't you, Dad?"

Before he could answer, Mrs. McGillicuddy walked over to her husband. "What in the world is that?"

"They are everywhere. Haven't you noticed?" Mr. McGillicuddy answered. "Just look around you."

And when she did, she said, "My gosh, how could I not have seen them?" In booth after booth, there were short ropes, long ropes, medium ropes, white ropes, and multicolored ropes. On each of them were anywhere from one to five Santa Claus figures, each of them looking like it was climbing to the top.

"Let me tell you about them, Grandma. And let me tell you how long they are going to be hanging off the balcony after we get home."

"What do you mean?"

"Just listen, Grandma. Christmas lasts a long time in Spain." And then he told her why as he hugged the two ropes filled with Santa Claus figures to his chest. When he finished, he said, "Okay, let's have the hot chocolate, and please, Daddy, can we buy the trees now?"

10

Two Trees to Decorate

The McGillicuddys, along with Remington and his parents, were having a special welcome-to-Spain dinner at Remington's favorite restaurant. It was very late at night, and some of the bulbs were ready to go to sleep.

"Hurry up, Bobby, and finish the story. I'm tired."

"Be patient, Bingo," Bobby answered.

"And will you explain to me why Remington is at a restaurant eating when he should already be asleep?"

"You better get used to this, Bingo, and all of you for that matter. I heard Remington tell Mr. and Mrs. McGillicuddy that most Spaniards don't have supper until at least ten o'clock, and some people go to restaurants as late as midnight."

"Bobby, get back to the story," his mom ordered. "Why is this tree and their other tree so small?"

"Like I told you. There just aren't large Christmas trees in Spain. At least that's what Remington told me when he pulled me out of his pocket and let me watch. They must have shopped at ten different Christmas tree booths in that big plaza.

"I didn't see all of the trees because whenever his parents or grandparents would turn to talk to him, he would quickly put me back in his pocket. But of the trees I saw, the largest ones weren't even half as tall as the trees the McGillicuddys have in their big room each year.

"Well this one certainly looks scrawny."

"What does scrawny mean, Mom?" Bobby's sister, Twinkle, asked.

Bobby's mom laughed and leaned forward. "Right there, Twinkle," she said and pointed with the tip of her nose. "See those big gaps? The branches aren't full and thick like the tree we've been on in Remington's room the past two years."

"One thing's for sure," Uncle Flicker's voice boomed loudly. "We'll be able to see each other this year. No one will be hidden."

"See, that means you can make something good out of almost anything," said Bobby's dad.

"What else did you see, Bobby?"

"Well, my dear little brother, there are some really different decorations and costumes the Spaniards wear during Christmas. And they also wear real funny-looking big wigs. Some are blue, some are red, lots of them are black, and I even saw some men with bright orange wigs. I think Remington's dad called them Afros.

"But the neatest thing I saw were long ropes that had Santa Clauses on them. They were hanging at almost every one of the booths that sell decorations. And on the way back here to the apartment, Remington had me out of his pocket most of the time. I saw lots of those ropes hanging from balconies. Here on the street where we are, every balcony had at least one Santa Claus rope hanging from it."

"Wow!" Energizer exclaimed. "They must really believe in Santa Claus in Spain."

Some of the bulbs laughed as Bobby continued. "If you can see out the window, you can just see the top of a Santa Claus hat hanging from that balcony rail across the street."

"Where are the two Santa Claus ropes the McGillicuddy's bought?" Sparkle asked.

"I'm not sure about the shortest one, but the longest one is on the balcony outside Remington's room, which is directly beneath us on the second floor. It has five different Santa Claus figures on it. It's nearly two stories long and goes all the way to the first floor."

"The first floor? What are you talking about? This is the first floor, right?"

"No, Aunt Glaring." Bobby turned in his pod to look at his aunt. "We are on the third floor. This is a big apartment. Remington and his parents each have a bedroom on the second floor, and the kitchen and living room are on the first floor, and then there is a ground floor where they get on the elevator to come upstairs."

"*Wow, this is a big place,*" chirped Uncle Glimmer from midway on the strand, but before he could finish what he wanted to say, the sound of Remington's voice echoed up the stairs from the floor below.

"*Looks like they are back from dinner,*" Bobby said.

"*What time is it, Bobby? Can you see the clock?*"

Bobby twisted and then turned back toward his mom. "*It's just past midnight.*"

"*And they just finished eating dinner,*" Bingo whined. "*That's unbelievable.*"

"*Quiet,*" Bobby whispered, and then the door opened and Mr. McGillicuddy entered the room.

"Did I just hear something in here?" Mr. McGillicuddy said as he threw open the door. He reached for the light switch, and when he flipped it on, his mouth flew open and he took a deep breath. "Oh my gosh! There's a Christmas tree in our room."

"Surprise, Grandpa," Remington said, and he burst into the room.

"What's going on?" Mrs. McGillicuddy said as she tromped in from the hallway. "What's that Christmas tree doing there?"

"Dad and I moved it in here after we got home while you guys were talking with Mom downstairs in the living room."

"But what about you? You need a tree. Isn't the other one we bought going to be in the living room?"

"Of course, Grandma. You saw it there. It's just that since you and Grandpa gave me my very own tree the last two years, Mom, Dad, and I thought you should get to have your own little tree here in your room in Madrid."

"Oh, Remington." Mrs. McGillicuddy started to cry. "You are the most wonderful grandson anyone could ever have, and your parents are the greatest too."

"Thank you," said Remington's mom. She and his father had just walked into the room.

"But it is not right." Mr. McGillicuddy tried to sound gruff, but he couldn't. Tears came to his eyes, and he reached down and pulled Remington up into his arms. He looked into his grandson's face. "You are a great kid, Remington. We would love to have this tree, but it needs to be in your room. We brought the bulbs so you could put them on your own tree again.

"Remember how I told you these bulbs were special and had helped save your grandma's life during the tornado?"

Before Remington could answer, Mrs. McGillicuddy said, "Oh, John, please. We don't need to go over that again."

"Gee, Dad," Remington's father said to Mr. McGillicuddy, "You sound like they jumped in the suitcase by themselves."

While the adults laughed, Remington reached over and ran his hands through the cord. Then he grabbed a blue bulb near the end of the strand and held it up with some of the other bulbs. "I know this is the same strand. This is definitely the blue bulb, Bobby."

"Remington, don't start that bulb talk again."

"Mom, it's true. You saw them yourselves last year. I heard you tell Daddy on the way home after Christmas that there was something mysterious about that strand of bulbs."

"Oh, I didn't really mean it."

"Oh yes you did."

"Well, forget all of that now," said Mr. McGillicuddy. "The important thing is you need to have the tree in your room so the bulbs can be closest to you."

"You mean it, Grandpa?"

"I mean it."

"So, is it okay if we move the tree, Mom? Is it, Dad?"

"It's okay."

It took ten minutes to bring the tree downstairs from the third floor to Remington's second-floor bedroom. Remington's dad placed it in the corner near the balcony window.

"Just leave everything, Richard. Remington will want to decorate the tree himself. He needs to be in bed. He'll be falling asleep in school tomorrow."

"I'm sure he's telling the folks some more about Christmas in Spain," he answered. "You know he is so excited that they are going to be here until January seventh, and he must have already explained to them at least three times that Christmas isn't over until January sixth.

"This is a great experience for him, dear, and his grandparents," she said and hugged her husband. "I'm glad your folks could come for Christmas. This should be one we remember forever."

"Not if I don't get some sleep. It's almost one o'clock."

Mr. McGillicuddy walked into the room carrying Remington in his arms. Mrs. McGillicuddy followed and placed her right index finger to her lips. She looked at Richard and Lisa. "Be real quiet; don't wake him up. I guess even after three months in Spain, he hasn't gotten used to staying up so late for dinner."

"No," Remington's mom said. "And really, he doesn't stay up this late normally."

Mr. McGillicuddy gently laid his grandson on the bed and pulled off his jacket and shoes. Remington didn't even stir, but he made everyone laugh when he suddenly snored loudly and rolled over on his stomach.

Mrs. McGillicuddy said, "Don't worry, John. Just let him sleep. He won't know whether he's wearing his pajamas or not." She reached down and turned a night light on next to his bed, and then all four of them slipped quietly into the hall.

"Good night, everyone," Mrs. McGillicuddy said and grabbed the arm of Mr. McGillicuddy and headed to the stairs.

"See you in the morning," Lisa said.

"Good night, folks," Richard said over his shoulder as he headed into their bedroom.

When Mr. McGillicuddy reached the door to the guest room on the third floor, he opened it for his wife. As she walked past him, he said, "Did you just say something?"

"No, dear; only you are hearing things."

"Very funny, Jane. I'm going to use the bathroom, and then I'll be ready for bed.

"Okay, but be quiet when you get back. I'll already be asleep."

Good, Mr. McGillicuddy thought, and he quietly walked through the hallway and down the stairs to Remington's room. He turned the overhead chandelier on for just a brief moment.

"I know something weird is going on with you bulbs. Just don't cause any problems." He stared directly at the blue bulb near the end of the strand. Then he yawned and leaned against the wall with his left shoulder.

"What's going on, Bobby? Are you awake?" His mom waited for a moment and then whispered again. *"Why are the lights turned on?"*

"Why are you talking?" Bobby's dad asked. *"I'm trying to sleep."*

"So am I," said Aunt Glaring.

Bobby whispered, "*Well, I'm wide awake and trying not to laugh out loud. Look up against the wall.*"

When the other three looked, they started laughing. In a matter of seconds, other bulbs began to wake up and soon they were also laughing as they stared at Mr. McGillicuddy, leaning up against the wall, snoring loudly.

11

An Amazing Christmas Pageant

In a country that is steeped in history with cities and towns filled with houses, public buildings, monuments, and statues often dating back as far as the tenth and eleventh century, there are few things that happen recently that are considered traditional.

However, there is one event, during the Christmas season in Madrid, which, because of its enormous popularity, has become a tradition in less than fifty years. It takes place at a very large department store named *El Corte Inglés*. This particular store on *Calle Preciados* is part of the largest chain of department stores in Spain. There are nearly a hundred stores, most in Spain, but some also in Portugal and other European countries.

They sell everything from clothes to cosmetics to furniture to books to appliances. The merchandise was similar to what you would find at a Macy's or Dillard's in America. But, at this particular *El Corte Inglés,* which is only a few blocks from the world-famous *Puerta Del Sol* in Madrid, there is an extraordinary Christmas pageant that features a different theme each year. Visitors from not only Madrid but also many other cities and small towns throughout Spain have made *Cortylandia* a part of their annual Christmas celebration.

From the first daily performance at eleven in the morning until the final one at 9:30 in the evening, well-dressed shoppers, daily workers, casual foreign visitors, along with homeless stragglers, all mingle side by side to view the show. Parents and grandparents bring their children. Neighbors schedule a meeting in front of the store, followed by a dinner at a nearby restaurant. Teen-agers make it the "thing to do" at least once each Christmas season.

Elbow to elbow, packed together like sardines in a can, they stand in a plaza, which is on the backside of the *Preciados* store. Every visitor to the show has one thing in common. They stand in awe as they look upward at the huge stage and the presentation.

Life-size figures of animals and humans mechanically move throughout the entire show with loud speakers blaring out their voices. All of this takes place on a stage that is nearly three stories high and actually sits attached to the side of the department store building.

For nearly half a century, hundreds of thousands of visitors have witnessed the extravaganza. And while people from every walk of life enjoy the show, it is groups of families that make up the largest part of the crowd at each performance. There is a reminder of that on a plaque attached to a large brick pillar at the store entrance. *Tus papas lo vieron siendo niños.*

"There is a special sign at the bottom of the building, right underneath where all the animals and human figures are, Grandma. I want you to see it because it explains how popular *Cortylandia* has become."

"Well, I'm sure looking forward to seeing it, if your daddy ever gets home from work."

Just then, the front door of the apartment opened on the floor below. "You just got your wish, Grandma." Remington jumped out of her lap. "I hear him downstairs. Go get Grandpa. We'll be leaving soon." Remington scooted out of the room, raced to the front door, and then hurried into the hall to greet his dad when he got off the elevator.

"How much farther is it?" It was the third time Mr. McGillicuddy had asked the question. The first time was when they had just reached the bottom of the hill, less than two blocks from the apartment. Then, just two blocks farther, as the group passed *Topolinos,* a favorite restaurant buffet of Remington and his parents, Mr. McGillicuddy had asked again.

Mrs. McGillicuddy stopped walking and looked at her husband. "Are you going to ask this question every two blocks until we get there?"

"Just wondering," Mr. McGillicuddy answered. "I'm just tired from walking around that museum all day."

"Come on, Grandpa." Remington ran up from behind Mr. McGillicuddy and grabbed him by the hand. "I'll pull you along and make it easier." Remington started to tug at his grandpa's hand, and they all laughed.

"Where were you, Remington?" his mom asked. Before he could answer, she continued, "You stay close to us. It's dark and too easy to get separated. In fact, you get in front of us and don't walk too fast."

"Oh, don't worry. I've got Grandpa with me. I can't walk fast." The others laughed, but Mr. McGillicuddy said nothing. "Just kidding, Grandpa," Remington said and looked up at him and winked. Then something flashed into Remington's mind.

It had been the wink that had done it. He had run down the stairs and given his dad a big hug, just moments after he had closed the front door. "Keep your coat on, Daddy. We'll be leaving for *Cortylandia* in just a few minutes." Then he had hurried back out of the living room and up the stairs, shouting over his shoulder, "I'm getting my coat and cap, Dad."

When he rushed into his room, he had walked by his Christmas tree without looking and had quickly opened the closet door. He grabbed the coat from a hanger and picked up his cap, which was lying on the floor. When he turned and closed the door, he glanced at the front of the tree across the room, and his mouth flew open.

"Remington, are you just going to stand there until we all freeze? It's cold. Why are you standing there staring across the street? Move it. Let's get going."

"What, Mom?"

"What's wrong with you? Are you okay?"

"Sure, Dad," Remington said. "I was just thinking of something."

"Well, think of it while we walk."

"Come on, Grandpa." Remington began pulling on Mr. McGillicuddy's hand. "We've got to hurry. The seven o'clock show begins in fifteen minutes."

"Now, suddenly you are in a hurry." Mrs. McGillicuddy laughed.

Remington tugged at Mr. McGillicuddy, and they started walking again. In less than half a block, the group turned the corner and entered a wide walkway that appeared to be a regular street but could only be used for pedestrian walking.

Calle de Preciados stretched all the way to the main plaza of *Puerta del Sol,* but they would be stopping before then. "Only about three or four minutes, and we'll be there," said Remington's dad.

Remington felt in the right pocket of his coat. His hand touched Bobby, and he remembered what had happened.

The lights weren't turned on, but it was still easy to see the bulbs. His eyes were focused on the spot at the very front of the tree. But something was wrong. The blue bulb was missing. The socket was empty.

"Oh my gosh! Where are you, Bobby?"

There were people walking shoulder to shoulder beneath large displays of red and white lights in the shape of poinsettias. They swayed back and forth in the wind above the pedestrian boulevard.

"Lots of Christmas shoppers out tonight," Remington's dad said.

"Just look at all these wonderful lights. I think these poinsettia lights are amazing, don't you, Lisa?"

Before she could answer, Remington's dad turned and said, "This is it. This is where we turn to walk to the rear of *El Corte Inglés.*"

Remington suddenly felt a tug on his left arm. "Your dad is telling you something," Mr. McGillicuddy said and then let out a deep sigh.

"What's wrong, Grandpa?"

"Oh, nothing. Just my feet are hurting."

Remington saw his dad just a few feet in front of him. He started to run up to him, but two teenagers came dashing in front of them and nearly collided with Mr. McGillicuddy.

"Oooh! Be careful there."

"Take it easy, Grandpa. They can't understand you."

Mr. McGillicuddy chuckled. "Teenagers. The same in every country."

"Here's where we turn," his dad said as Remington skipped up beside him.

"I know. Right down this little street and we're there."

They entered the narrow side street. "Everybody stay close together," Remington's dad shouted over his shoulder.

"Wow! Look at the size of this crowd, Grandpa," Remington shouted as the five of them reached the end of the street and turned into the plaza.

"Oh my goodness. Are we really going to walk into that mass of people?"

"Don't worry, Grandpa. We'll be fine."

Before Remington could say anything else, his dad interrupted. "Let's all talk this over. It's so crowded; I think we should try to get to the rear of the crowd and stand underneath that walkway." He pointed to an office building across the plaza with a second-floor balcony.

As they headed through the crowd, Remington felt once more in his pocket and touched Bobby. He smiled and remembered how surprised he had been when he had gone into his bedroom to get the bulb.

"What's going on? How did you get out of that socket?" Remington walked quickly to the tree and looked down on the narrow front branch.

"How did you get loose? I know I put you back in your socket when we came back from selecting the Christmas trees."

At that moment the blue bulb winked at Remington.

Remington was directly behind his dad and reached for his hand as the people around them pushed and shoved. "You hold on to me tight." Then his dad yelled to the other three, "Come on; we are almost to the walkway."

As they pushed the final few feet and stepped into an area where there was actually no one standing, they heard theme song music for the start of the performance. "Hear the music?" Remington looked up at his granddad and shouted. "That means the show is about to begin."

Remington turned and quickly pulled the bulb out of his pocket. He winked at it and put the bulb up close to his lips. "Get ready for some real fun, Bobby. I'll hold you up in the air, if I can, so you can see the show."

"What did you say, Remington?" his dad shouted above the music and the chattering of Spanish that surrounded them.

"Nothing, Dad," Remington lied. "Just telling Mom and Grandpa and Grandma to stay close." Then Remington thought to himself, *Well, it's not really a lie. I was thinking that at least.*

The McGillicuddy family was lined up against the grayish stonewall of a sixteenth-century building across the plaza and opposite of *El Corte Inglés*. Hundreds and hundreds of spectators were jammed together at least thirty to forty rows deep. All eyes were staring upward at the wide gate at the front of the stage. There were guardhouses on each side of the two swinging sections of the gate. Above the gate was a huge sign that read, "*El Zoo de Cortylandia.*"

It had now been dark for over an hour, but there were rays of light from the department store windows splashing upon the crowd. The streetlights at the corners of the plaza added some more brightness.

As the background music that had been playing for the past fifteen minutes began to fade away, Mrs. McGillicuddy laughed and looked at her husband. "See, John," she said and pointed with the index finger of her right hand toward the department store. "I know some Spanish too. It says the *'Zoo at Cortylandia,'*" she said proudly.

Remington was talking with his folks at the moment, and the McGillicuddys had a rare moment to visit without their grandson explaining what was going on. "It really is an amazing job what they have done in constructing all of this on the side of the building," said Mr. McGillicuddy.

"I know," said Mrs. McGillicuddy, "and Richard says they change it every year."

"Look at all the different types of animal figures. Everything from giraffes, tigers, elephants, lions, and, gorillas. It's quite a zoo."

"It's an amazing selection," Mrs. McGillicuddy said. "I mean, not just wild animals, but that huge cage must be twenty-five feet high. Look at all the different exotic bird figures they have created. It's an excellent job. The parrots and toucans actually look real."

"Almost all of the animals do," he agreed. "The only things that don't are those toy-like soldiers and the guard near the front gate."

Mrs. McGillicuddy noticed Remington had walked away from his parents, and because it wasn't quite as crowded where they were standing, he was leaning against the building, patiently waiting. "What are they singing, Richard?" Mrs. McGillicuddy asked her son.

"I'm not sure, Mom. Some of the songs are too hard for me to understand."

"Listen." Remington tugged at the leg of his grandfather. "They are getting ready to begin."

Before he could say anything else, there was a loud noise, much like the clap of thunder. A collective gasp of air came from the crowd. Spotlights immediately splashed across the side of the building, spreading light across the entire stage. Another rush of oohs and aahs came from the mouths of the spectators below.

Then came the sounds of trumpets blaring, and the audience became silent. Within seconds, a peppy song punctuated by a chorus of words being sung in Spanish caused the crowd to cheer loudly.

Now the large gate began to slowly open. Behind the gate on each side were two figures dressed very similar to what a doorman at a hotel would wear.

They were the guards. From one of them came the words, "*Bienvenidos a Cortylandia.*"

"That means 'Welcome to *Cortylandia*,' Grandma," Remington yelled.

Just then, the crowd let out a loud cheer as the trunk of the elephant standing behind the open gate flew up into the air and there was a bellowing sound before he said, "*Despiertan.*" The crowd started laughing. "Let me tell them, Daddy," Remington said before his father could say a word. "He just told everybody to wake up," Remington squealed, and his grandparents joined in the laughter.

"Oh, this is so sweet, Lisa. What a wonderful experience, even though I won't be able to understand a word," said Mrs. McGillicuddy.

Now the music got much louder, and everyone standing around them began to sway back and forth. Locked arm in arm, the Spaniards moved from side to side for nearly half a minute. The group of bodies, swishing to and fro, looked like large ocean waves heading into shore. Only these waves were wearing winter coats and hats and were smiling.

Then, as the music began to soften, the movement slowed down, and the crowd began to sing. Remington tugged at the leg of Mr. McGillicuddy and shouted up at him. "Tell Grandma that this is the *Cortylandia* theme song. They will sing it again when the show is over."

While Mr. McGillicuddy passed on the message, Remington reached deep in his pocket and brought the bulb out. Then, holding it in the air so his parents and grandparents couldn't see the bulb, he and Bobby Bright watched the amazing display of talking mechanical animals, birds, and human beings.

Fifteen minutes later, the final song was being sung. The mouths of the two giraffes moved in unison, and they sang as they stretched their long necks to the right. Then they stopped and the song continued from the mouths of three elephants, a huge white gorilla, and two rhinoceros. As they moved in unison, the crowd laughed loudly.

"Oh, what a great night," Mrs. McGillicuddy said to her son and daughter-in-law, who were standing next to her.

"It really is a great show," Lisa said. "This is the third time we've seen it. Richard understands some of the words of the song, and whenever the animals talk he can understand most of it. Even though Remington and I don't understand a lot of what's being said, we enjoy it too."

Remington shoved his way between the two of them and looked up at his grandmother. "I know quite a bit of the words, Grandma," he said.

"Oh, I know you do." She smiled at her grandson. "And when we get back to the apartment you can tell me some of the things that were said."

"Listen, everybody." Lisa raised her voice so she could be heard. There were stares from the people standing in front of them as they turned to see who was speaking a foreign language. "We need to stay close together because when the show ends in about thirty seconds, there will be lots of people trying to get out of this square quickly."

She started to continue, but Remington's dad interrupted. "What are you doing, Remington? Get back over here close to us."

"I know what I'm doing. I've been here before."

"Listen to me, Remington McGillicuddy," his mom snapped. You are nine years old. You will stay close to us. Do you understand?"

"Yes, Mom," Remington whined.

"If any of us get separated from the others," she continued, "don't panic. Just continue to walk straight ahead toward the steps of the department store. It will be easy to find each other standing in front of that main door." She pointed over the top of the crowd. "Do you see the front of the store?"

"Yes, dear," said Mrs. McGillicuddy, "I see it fine."

"We'll be okay," added Mr. McGillicuddy "if we just hold hands. We won't get lost."

But he was very wrong about that.

12

Lost in Madrid

It was less than ten minutes since the music had stopped and the show had ended. And no one could understand how this could have happened so quickly. Remington's mom was crying. Her son was missing.

"How did this happen?" she screamed at her husband.

She buried her head on the shoulder of Mrs. McGillicuddy, who had tears streaming down the front of her face. The two women hugged, and to the side, Remington's dad and Mr. McGillicuddy stared at each other in disbelief.

"He knows to come here to the store. He will be okay," Remington's dad said, but his voice didn't sound like he meant it.

"Oh, Richard, my baby is lost."

"What are we going to do?" Mr. McGillicuddy asked Richard.

"Stay here. I just saw a policeman step inside those revolving doors. I will be right back."

It had happened so quickly. Just like that, his family was gone. Tears began to stream down his cheeks as he thought back to just a couple of minutes earlier.

"I've got your hand, Grandpa, but I need to get something out of my pocket." It was then he had pulled his hand loose and reached into his pocket to grab Bobby. When he looked up, there were five people directly in front of him. They were barely moving as the crowd inched forward. A mother and father in front of him were trying to hold onto the hands of their three children.

Remington wiped the tears with the back of his left hand. He held the bulb in his right hand. Suddenly he thought he saw his family. "There they are, Bobby," Remington said and looked at the bulb in his hand.

At that moment, two Madrid teenagers started laughing and pointing at Remington. "*Está loco!*" Then they both laughed.

He understood what they had said and shouted back, "I am not crazy." But he was scared, and he was definitely lost. He remembered what his dad had told him more than once. "Don't panic. That's the most important thing. Remember to try and be calm."

The boys had already disappeared around a corner. Remington hurried after them and entered a very small street filled with lots of restaurants and *tapas* bars. There were still lots of people on the streets and most were in a hurry to go eat. His mom and dad had promised him they would take Grandpa and Grandma to one of the family's favorite restaurants near the *Plaza Mayor* after seeing *Cortylandia*.

As Remington thought of his family, he started crying once more. He was standing to one side of a small plaza that looked familiar to him. He was sure he and his parents had walked through this area many times before.

As he leaned back against the window of a bookstore, tears rolled down his cheeks. People rushed by without paying him any attention. Remington stared across the small plaza. He thought he recognized a building. However, seconds later, as he wiped away the tears, he was pretty sure he and his family had not been in this plaza that night.

Ten minutes later, he was still crying. He was shaking, not only from the chill of the night, but also because he was very frightened. He took Bobby back out of his pocket and held the bulb in his hand. He looked at it, and when he didn't see anyone close enough to see him, he said, "This isn't the same square in front of the department store. But we'll be okay, Bobby. I'll get us back to *El Corte Inglés*."

It was at that moment Remington spotted a small bench sitting on the cobblestone sidewalk directly in front of a large restaurant. He ran to it and jumped up on top of the bench so he could see beyond the plaza. He stood on his tiptoes and at first almost fell off the bench as he tried to keep his balance.

There were two small streetlights a half a block away. The street was very dark, and he couldn't see anyone who looked like his parents or grandparents. He began sobbing even louder. He started quivering. The more he shook, the harder it was to catch his breath. Now, there were only a few people walking past him, and most were teenagers who paid him no attention.

"I'm scared, Bobby," Remington said, and he cried even louder. "I'm lost in Madrid."

She was old, and her clothes were way too big for her. They hung off her shoulders, and her dress was clear down to her ankles. She had on a small scarf that covered very dirty hair, and as she got closer, Remington could tell she had not had a bath in a long time. She was a "*gente de la calle.*"

Remington's dad had warned him when they had first moved into an apartment near the center of downtown,

"You will see homeless street people. Sometimes they can be dangerous if bothered."

Están sin vivienda. Remington was studying Spanish and still had a lot to learn, but his dad had explained, "Those words mean 'they are without a home.'"

He saw her shuffling toward him with tiny steps. *Está sin vivienda.* He was sure of that. He panicked and ran to the end of the corner. Behind him, in the distance, he heard her shout, "*¿Por qué llore, niño? Por qué llore?*"

As soon as he turned the corner, he stopped and pulled the bulb from his pocket. "I'm so scared, Bobby," he said and stared at the bulb for a moment. Then he looked up, and in front of him was a very long, wide street. There were no cars. It was like the *Calle de Preciados,* where he and his family had walked earlier in the evening, but he knew it was not the same street. That street had been well lit, almost like daylight, even when it was night-time. But here it was darker, even though there were tall streetlight poles. The giant globes hung so high above the ground that there were many shadowy areas on the walkway.

In the distance, he could just make out small groups of people standing and talking. He could also see two or three families walking together. Children, just like him, were holding the hands of their moms and dads. But nowhere in sight was his family.

"Oh, Bobby," Remington whined, and he thought he would start crying again. Then he stood up straight and once more looked at the bulb. "You are my friend. Please help me." Remington waited, but nothing happened. He stood there, fighting off the tears that were again rolling from his eyes.

"Please, someone help me," he said, but there was no one to hear him. He started to yell for help but then stopped and stared in disbelief. At that moment, he discovered what a magical friend he had in the tiny bulb laying in his hand.

He would always believe from this moment on that it was true what his grandparents had told him about the bulbs saving his grandmother from a tornado last year. And he would always know for certain that it had been Bobby who had saved him from a terrible Christmas Eve accident a year ago.

13

The Rescue

Remington stared in disbelief. He looked at his empty hand, and then he looked into the darkness above him. He started to scream but didn't because two groups of people talking loudly were walking past. He understood nothing they were saying.

What he did understand was that he had just seen something miraculous. He had watched Bobby spin free from his hand, escape, and fly away. The bulb was twirling so fast he could barely see it as it became smaller and smaller and disappeared into the darkness.

Bobby was spinning so fast he could barely see what was below him. For a moment he thought about what he had just done. He had so wanted to say to Remington, "Stay here, Remington. Don't move. I'll find your parents."

But of course, that was impossible. He could barely say his own name in human language, let alone two whole sentences. He could only hope Remington was smart enough to stay where he was and wait for help.

Remington could no longer see the flying bulb. He stood there alone, staring down the street. There were more people walking toward him. He wondered if they were coming from *Cortylandia*.

"*Whiiist! Whiist!*" Remington turned when he heard the whistles. What he saw frightened him.

Those same two teenage boys who had yelled something at him earlier had returned and were walking toward him. "*¿Habla a tu mismo?*" They laughed.

Remington turned to run, and then he heard and saw her at the same time. The old lady with the tattered and dirty clothes was limping toward him. She was yelling something at the two boys.

They turned and looked at her. Then they laughed and pointed. "*Vieja sucia.*" They screamed again at the old woman. The words sounded the same to Remington. He understood *vieja. She definitely was old,* he thought.

Then he watched in astonishment. She kept limping toward the boys, and the two teenagers suddenly weren't so brave, and they turned and yelled lots of words at her. Remington thought they were trying to act brave, but now he knew they weren't. He even laughed as the teenagers put two fingers on each side of their noses, like something didn't smell good. Then they walked away.

The old woman kept hobbling toward him. He was glad she had scared away the two boys, but he was still afraid of her. Remington turned and ran only four or five steps up the wide avenue before he stopped. She had made a strange-sounding, high-pitched scream that put shivers down his back.

He turned and saw her standing with her right hand over her eyes. Her left hand was pointed in the air, and she was still screaming. Remington turned back around to see what she was pointing at. When he looked upward into the darkness, he got a glimpse of something sailing through the air, barely visible as it flew in between the rays of light shining from the tall street lamps. Suddenly he realized what it was, and he shouted too, but in excitement.

Bobby looked back just once as he flew away from Remington. He had been slightly surprised that he had managed enough power to escape Remington's hand. He had done so whispering twice, "*Puhrumba! Puhrumba!*"

He knew he wouldn't have much time until his power would begin to disappear, and he would weaken. In the distance, at least two blocks away, he could see more light. He just wanted to get someplace where there were more people and maybe find the McGillicuddy family.

He could only get about twelve to fifteen feet in the air, so he stayed close to the buildings so the people walking below would have less chance to see him. He had no idea what those Spaniards would do if they saw a bulb flying in the air, but he sure didn't want to find out.

It had been about thirty seconds since he had escaped Remington's hand. The brighter lights were getting closer, and he began to see lots of people standing shoulder to shoulder. As he continued forward, he felt for the first time, a slight loss of his power. He knew he must hurry, and he realized he would need to be lucky for something to happen. It was at that moment he saw a familiar sight.

Less than a block in front of him was the giant sign that Remington, his family, and the huge crowd had been staring up at earlier in the evening. As he drew closer to the plaza, he reduced his power and the speed of his rotation. He maneuvered into the shadows of a nearby building.

There was no doubt. He recognized the two toy soldier guards placed on each side of the gate. He had no idea what the sign meant in Spanish, but he definitely knew it was the same one. But none of this would mean anything if he couldn't find the McGillicuddys. He had to hurry.

He was losing power. From the back edge of the plaza he saw another crowd gathering for the final *Cortylandia* performance of the evening.

He was unable to recognize anyone on the steps of the department store. He knew he couldn't get any closer. *What will happen,* he thought to himself, *if I am spotted by anyone? Will they shoot me down? Will they throw something at a spinning bulb in the air, or will they scream and run away?* Bobby laughed at the thought.

Now another thought entered his mind. *What if none of Remington's family is still here?* It was possible they might already be searching in another part of downtown Madrid.

There was a sudden loud clamoring noise, which interrupted his thoughts. The noise shook the square. It was the sound of someone tapping on the edge of a microphone, and large loudspeakers squealed and made weird sounds. Then he heard a voice in Spanish begin to speak. "*Atención. Escúchenme, ¡por favor!*"

After a loud murmuring among the spectators, slowly the crowd became quiet. The voice continued, but Bobby couldn't understand anything. As the speaker continued, Bobby felt weaker and weaker and knew he had to get back to Remington. He was afraid he might crash to the sidewalk below.

He was so disappointed. He had actually found the plaza and the place where Remington had been separated from his folks, and yet he couldn't find them. He twisted and increased his rotation and started to leave when he suddenly reversed his rotation one more time and spun in space. For the briefest moment he thought he saw a familiar face. He leaned forward and looked across the square again.

The crowd was no longer pushing and shoving and moving about. They were standing in place, and everyone stared upward at the speakers as the Spanish voice continued to blare down upon the crowd. It was easier to recognize faces and that was exactly what had happened.

Bobby saw them. There they were. Policemen were surrounding them, but he knew it was the McGillicuddys and Remington's folks. He could see Remington's dad waving his hands and talking with two of the policemen who looked older and had on police uniforms that were different from the others.

Then as the voice in Spanish continued on, Bobby recognized just one word from all that was being said. When he did, cold chills ran down his filaments. His eyes watered, and he knew what was happening. Then he heard the word repeated again, the only word he understood: Remington.

The police were announcing something to the crowd, and they had said Remington. It must mean they were reporting to the crowd that there was a boy named Remington who was lost. And then he knew for sure, when he heard the word *Americano*.

"Well, they won't find him here," Bobby said to himself. He changed his midair rotation and increased his power. Now he ducked his head forward and began flying back the way he had come. Staying in the nighttime shadows and near the side of the buildings, he flew as fast as his weakening power would allow. He could only hope Remington had stayed where he had left him.

Remington was scared. The old woman limped toward him. She was yelling at him in Spanish. She spoke too fast. Remington couldn't understand anything.

What he did understand was that Bobby was gone. He had flown right out of his hand. How could his bulb buddy do this? Why would he leave him all alone?

Now the woman was only a few feet away. He could smell her, and her face was scarred and covered with red bumps. He screamed, "¡Ayúdame! ¡Por favor, ayúdame!"

He remembered his mom and dad telling him right after they had moved to Madrid that if he were ever in trouble and they weren't near to yell those words. "Please help me," he said in English. And then he ran away from the old woman, up the dark avenue.

Remington ran as hard as he could. He looked over his shoulder. The old woman tried to keep up, but she was too slow, and her voice screaming in the distance finally could no longer be heard. People walking in the middle of the wide avenue looked toward the running boy. A couple of them yelled something at him, but he didn't understand and wouldn't have stopped anyway. He just continued to run in the direction he had seen Bobby fly.

Tears streamed down his face, but he didn't want to yell for help because he didn't know any of these people. He just wanted his mom and dad and his grandparents and his best buddy, Bobby.

"Where are you, Bobby?" he shouted louder than he had ever shouted before.

And then he looked up, and his question was answered.

Bobby didn't know if he could reach Remington before his power ran out. In fact, Bobby didn't know if Remington would even be where he had left him. His rotation was less than half of what it had been, and he felt himself dropping down toward the sidewalk.

"Oh, Remington," Bobby said to himself. "I don't know if I can get back to you."

But Bobby didn't have to go any farther.

Remington kept running and at the same time tried to wipe away his tears with his right hand. He approached a corner and stopped for a moment. He looked both ways down the street that crossed the walking avenue. To his right, the street slanted downward. At the far end of that hill were a few people, but they were walking away from him. That was good, because he was frightened and didn't want to be near anyone.

He took a few steps down the street, and as he peered over the crest of the street where it dropped downward, he thought he recognized a building with a lot of lights shining on it. He started to go on down the street, but something made him turn his head for a moment. "Oh my gosh!" he screamed.

What he saw made him feel like his heart had jumped out of his body. "It's you, Bobby."

Bobby dropped down to only three or four feet above the sidewalk and spun in place as he watched Remington run toward him. Bobby saw a young Spanish couple. Each of them was pushing a baby carriage.

They looked toward Remington, and the man started to walk toward him but turned back when he heard the voice of his wife.

Bobby began releasing his power. As he started to fall, Remington yelled, "Be careful, Bobby." Then Remington plucked him out of the air and squeezed him into his hand.

"Why did you leave me, Bobby?" Remington said as he peered down at the blue bulb in his hand. "Oh, I wish you could talk to me. What am I going to do?"

Before Remington could say anything else, he heard the voice again, and he turned and saw her. The old woman was limping toward him, and the smell was back. "*¡Niño! ¡Espéreme! ¡Espéreme, por favor!*"

Remington turned and started to run, but then he stopped. The bulb had fallen from his hand. He screamed, "No, Bobby. You will break." And as he reached for it, hoping to catch it before it hit the pavement, his hand froze in midair, and his mouth flew open again. Just before the bulb was about to hit the cobblestone pavement, it spun so fast that Remington couldn't even recognize its color. It flew right past his nose and up into the air where it spun in a circle five feet above him.

"What are you doing? Don't leave me again," yelled Remington.

But Bobby leaned forward in midair, flew just a few feet, and then he turned and flew back above Remington. When Remington jumped into the air to try and catch him, the bulb flew away again, only to stop and then turn and come back. It was then, as Remington stared above him, he figured out what Bobby was trying to do. He wanted Remington to follow him.

That was an easy decision when Remington looked to his left and saw the old woman was only five feet away. Even in the dim light from the street lamp above, he could see the rips and tears in her dress and how worn and beaten her shoes were. He turned and chased after Bobby as the bulb flew close to the buildings in front of him. In the distance, Remington saw some lights. They were just a couple of blocks away.

"You finally understand, Remington," Bobby whispered to himself as he looked down at the little redhead running and waving his hands up at him. *"Two more blocks,"* Bobby said as he looked ahead and saw the edge of the huge crowd gathered in the plaza.

He could once more hear the noise from the loud-speakers. He was certain it was not music or the voices from the presentation Remington and his family had watched earlier. He was certain it was the same voice he had heard just minutes ago that had said, "Remington."

They were within a block of the square. In less than a minute, there would no longer be a need for announcements about a little boy being lost.

"Is there any word, Richard? I am so frightened. Can't we just go look for him?"

"Honey, let's wait ten more minutes. The officer told me he has policemen walking every side street off the plaza and beginning to ask people if they have seen anyone who looks like Remington."

"But, why can't we try to find him? You go with your mom, and I'll go with your dad. We can stay together in pairs, plus we can call each other on our cell phones."

"Let's do that, Richard." It was Mrs. McGillicuddy. She had her head on the chest of Mr. McGillicuddy as the four stood close together directly beneath one of the loudspeakers. From time to time they heard the mention of Remington's name.

"Alright, let me tell Officer Saludo that we are going to go try and look for him."

Remington suddenly recognized where he was. "It's the plaza. It's *El Corte Inglés*," he shouted, and an elderly couple turned to look at him. They were standing at the back of the huge crowd in front of the department store. Remington looked up and saw Bobby drop down toward him and land in his hand.

"*Dios mio*," the man and woman screamed in unison as they pointed at the bulb that had just fallen from beneath the balcony, a bulb that they were certain had just been spinning in the air by itself.

The couple screamed even louder, and now other people began to turn their heads. They saw the two people pointing toward the shadows of the building. And then as if some powerful giant had reached down and pushed half the crowd one way and the other half the opposite way, the huge gathering separated.

More people began to shout. "*El pelirrojo. El pelirrojo.*"

Remington's dad whistled and raised his hand and circled it in the air. The police officer in charge of the search heard and turned to walk toward the American but then stopped immediately. From the far side of the plaza, he heard voices, and they were all screaming the same thing. "*El Pelirrojo, El Pelirrojo.*"

The officer and Richard McGillicuddy now were within a few feet of each other, and they stared at each other and both realized at the same time what was happening. "I think he found, señor," the Spanish police lieutenant said in his broken English.

"*Se fue encontrado,*" Remington's dad shouted back. And then the two of them began to push and shove their way through the crowd.

Behind them, Remington's mom screamed to Mr. and Mrs. McGillicuddy. "They found him. I know enough

Spanish to know. I just heard the word *redhead*. They have found my baby."

Remington stood with his eyes wide open. The crowd had parted, and in the distance he saw a police officer running and behind him was another man. And then Remington knew who it was.

"Daddy!" he shouted and started running. The people on both sides of an aisle that had parted the huge crowd began to applaud. They started a sharp whistling noise that was popular in Spain when something exciting or thrilling had happened.

And as Remington ran toward his dad, he clutched Bobby tightly in his hand. Seconds later, he jumped into his father's arms, and he hugged him as hard as he could. He looked over his dad's shoulders, and he saw his mom and grandparents running toward him. The noise was amazing. People were clapping their hands and whistling throughout the square. He got down out of his dad's arms and ran toward his mom. The people continued to clap, cheer, and whistle.

But then suddenly the crowd began to get quiet. And voices were heard yelling, "*¡Mira! ¡Mira! ¡Mira!*" People started pointing to the path that separated both sides of the crowd.

The object of the pointing was the old woman. She was hobbling and trying to catch up with Remington. She screamed loudly, and the police lieutenant and two more policemen started to grab her, but then they stopped. They stared at her, and others in the crowd did the same. Some people were holding their noses. A quiet came over the crowd as she screamed, "*Es Diablo. Es un fantasma. Hay encanto magia sobre este niño y su bombilla. Tiene un foco de navidad mágico.*"

The crowd was silent for a moment, and then laughter began to come from all sides of the woman. People began to point and laugh even louder. "*Una bombilla mágica. Loco, loco, loco.*"

As Remington's mom hugged him as hard as she could, and Mr. and Mrs. McGillicuddy were bending over and trying to squeeze him at the same time, the crowd continued to laugh and shout, "*Loco, loco, loco.*" Finally Remington pulled loose and shouted, "She tried to catch me. I was afraid of her, Mom."

"What do you mean she tried to catch you?"

"She smells terrible, and she had dirty clothes, and she kept running toward me and yelling something about niño."

Remington started to tell his mom more but stopped and stared at the woman. The police had taken her by both arms and were walking her toward Remington's dad and the policeman standing next to him.

Remington saw his dad grab his nose and pinch it as the woman got near. And then Remington watched as she gestured with her hands. She kept circling her hands in the air and pointing to the sky, and then she would turn and point back at Remington. It was then he realized what she was trying to explain.

14

What Really Happened

"What really happened, Remington? We will be quiet, and you tell us how you got lost and how you found your way back to us. And please, no more stories like that crazy old woman just told the police."

"But it is the truth, Mom. That is what happened. Bobby saved me."

"Remington McGillicuddy! I promised myself I wouldn't scold you when we found you because we love you so much, and we were so scared. However, I am not going to listen to another bulb story about Bobby. You can keep him on your tree, you can claim he's told you his name, and you can even sneak him off the tree like you have been doing. You can take him with you when we go places, but you are not going to tell me he flew around in the air and led you back to the square."

Remington sat there staring at his mom. They were in the living room of their apartment, and his dad and grandparents were just sitting there saying nothing. He looked at all of them. "You don't want to believe me. You don't want to believe that old dirty woman. But," he continued, "she told the truth."

His mom started to say something, but Remington's dad interrupted her. "Just a minute, honey. Think back, Remington, to the moment you first saw her."

Remington looked at his dad with a blank look on his face, and after a few moments, his eyes got brighter. "I remember now, Dad. The very first time was in that tiny little square with the restaurant. Remember, I told you on the way home. I think it was a restaurant where we had eaten once before. Well, anyway, right in front of the restaurant was where those two teenage boys I told you about acted like they were going to grab me."

"They started to hurt you?" Mrs. McGillicuddy spoke for the first time since they had gotten to the apartment.

"They were at least saying something and laughing and pointing at me. I was scared."

Then Remington got quiet. He sat there staring at the living room ceiling. Four sets of eyes were looking at him. His mom, dad, grandma, and grandpa all waited to hear more.

He was silent for nearly half a minute. They waited patiently, but finally his dad leaned forward and started to speak, but Remington continued. "You know, Dad, I do remember now. It was the second time those teenage boys started yelling at me. They came back later after I had left that little square. They looked like they might come over and grab me, and that's when I saw her again. In fact, you know what?" Remington paused once more and stared at the television set on the other side of the room.

When he said nothing for ten seconds, Remington's dad gently whispered, "Go ahead, Remington. Think and tell us what happened."

"So then, Bobby, what else did he say?" It was his cousin, Flash, who asked the question.

"Well, what Remington said was this. He told his parents and Mr. and Mrs. McGillicuddy that he had finally realized something very important. He admitted he was wrong about the old woman. He told his folks that even though she was dirty, smelled awful, and was covered with red bumps, bruises, and scars, she was probably a good person."

Bobby paused for a moment so his family could think about what he had said and then continued, "You see, the only thing that old woman wanted to do, once she had chased those teenage boys away, was to try and help him. She had asked him why he was crying. She had tried to get him to stop and not run away from her. But Remington was too scared, and he didn't realize what she was saying."

Then Bobby stopped talking and looked around the tree to make sure all of his relatives were listening.

Just as he started to continue, he heard Dazzling. "Well, Robert, are you going to keep it a secret or tell us what happened and how brave you are?"

Bobby started to answer his snooty little cousin, but Aunt Glaring spoke first. "Dazzling, you be quiet. Leave him alone. Bobby isn't bragging; he is just trying to tell his story."

"Oh, Mom," she whined and started to say more, but Bobby interrupted her.

"She said she saw something that looked like a bulb flying in the air, and then she screamed and went running after Remington. Remington's dad said the police reported that she thought at first the thing she saw was a tiny bird or a baby bat."

Bobby's brother, Dimmer, interrupted him. "So, does that mean if you foul up and make a mistake in the future"—he paused and chuckled—"that I get to call you dingbat?"

No one said anything for a moment, and then suddenly laughter came from all parts of the tree. Bobby waited for everyone to get quiet before he shouted, "Okay, Dimmer. You got me this time. That's a good one. From now on when I make a mistake, I am your dingbat brother."

"I have a better idea," Sparkle said. "How about Hero Dingbat?"

It must have been a good idea because all of the bulbs cheered and applauded.

15
Gifts for the Needy

It was eleven thirty. "I cannot believe this." Mrs. McGillicuddy yawned and looked across the dining room table. "I have never eaten this late since those days in college when you and I would go have a snack after we had studied in the library, John."

Mr. McGillicuddy started to answer, but Remington quickly said, "I eat this late all the time."

"You don't eat this late," his mom said. "We normally eat at eight o'clock. You know that. We've eaten at that time ever since we got here."

Remington started to say something, but his mom continued, "I will admit that sometimes on the weekend, when we eat dinner at a restaurant, we don't go until ten or ten thirty. It is just so common here."

"Well, Mom, you definitely should be hungry after all the excitement this evening."

"If she's not, I certainly am," said Mr. McGillicuddy.

"Grandpa, you are always hungry," said Remington. Just as everyone started laughing, the phone rang.

Everyone was eating oven-baked chicken, and Mr. and Mrs. McGillicuddy were very delicately picking among some fried calamari on their plate when Remington's dad came back into the room.

"Is there something wrong at the embassy?" Remington's mom asked.

"No, that was the police station up the hill. They wanted to let me know that nothing was being done to the old woman. They have washed her off, at least the best they can do at the precinct station, and are going to let her stay in a cell overnight. It will be the warmest night she'll have this winter."

"Oh, Richard," Mrs. McGillicuddy said. She looked across the table at her son. "You mean she lives on the street?"

"I told you that right after the police hauled her away in front of *El Corte Inglés.*"

"I know, but I thought she must have a shelter or something."

"She might. You know, as marvelous as Madrid is, there still are places on the *Gran Via,* probably the widest and most historical street in all of Spain, where the police let homeless people crawl under cardboard boxes and lean-to shelters. You saw some of them tonight when we were walking to see *Cortylandia.* They are right there on the steps of some of the buildings."

"Oh my goodness." Mrs. McGillicuddy gasped. "You mean she lives in one of those?"

"I don't know, but it's possible. Now, let's quit talking about this and enjoy the meal."

"Listen to me, Richard," Mrs. McGillicuddy said, "we will finish this lovely dinner, even though it is late. But I will tell you two things. I am no longer sleepy, and that woman is not leaving that police station wearing those filthy clothes again."

"What are you talking about?" Mr. McGillicuddy looked up at his wife, and when he did, juice from the rotisserie chicken rolled down his chin.

"What I'm talking about is that when I finish this last bite of chicken, I am going to get my suitcase out of the closet. I am going to find those extra two dresses I brought with me in case any of the other clothes were damaged. I am going to take those dresses to that woman. The first thing I noticed about her, behind all that dirt, all those scars, and all those bumps, was a woman like me."

"Like you?" Mr. McGillicuddy gulped. "Why, Jane, you are crazy."

"No. I'm not. She is my same size, and once all those dirty old tattered clothes are removed, she will fit into those dresses. And, most likely, she is my age. After hearing how she wanted to help Remington, I think she is very much a woman like me. I am going to the police station."

Remington's mom interrupted. "Are you sure you want to do that right now?"

"Oh, yes, Lisa. I'm very sure." And with that statement, Mrs. McGillicuddy left the room.

16

A Surprise for Bobby and His Family

It was early Monday morning. Remington rode to school in the car with his dad, who had then gone on to the U.S. embassy. Mr. and Mrs. McGillicuddy were so exhausted from all of the excitement from the night before and staying up until two o'clock in the morning that they had slept late.

When they came downstairs to the kitchen, Lisa was cooking some scrambled eggs. "Good morning," she said. "You two look a lot better than last night." She laughed and continued. "In fact, we all do. We were a tired bunch of people when we got back from that police station."

"Have you heard anything yet, Lisa?" Mrs. McGillicuddy asked.

"Well, Richard told me before he left an hour ago that the police had called at 8:30 and told him they had released the woman. They told him she was wearing one of the new dresses you left for her. In fact, the police said she threw the two old dresses and that horrible-looking sweater in the trash bin outside the police station before she left and hobbled down the street.

"Well, I can only hope she is at least a little happier than she was," said Mrs. McGillicuddy. "I only wish we could have done more."

"What do you want to do?" Mr. McGillicuddy asked. "Should we invite her to come live with us?"

"John McGillicuddy, don't you be mean. There is nothing funny about that."

"Sorry, dear," he mumbled and quickly changed the subject as he reached for the platter filled with eggs and bacon. "Lisa, this is just like being in the States. Eggs and bacon."

"What do you think about the bacon, Dad? Do you think it tastes much different?"

"Yes, but it tastes darn good too." He handed the plate of bacon to his wife. "Try some of that bacon, Jane." But Mrs. McGillicuddy didn't reach for the plate. She just stared at him and said nothing. "Are you all right?" he asked.

She still just stared into space.

"Jane, are you okay?"

"Oh, yes," she said. "Sorry, I was just thinking about that poor woman."

"Mom," Lisa interrupted, "forget about her. It is difficult, but there is nothing you can do."

Remington's mom couldn't have been more wrong, as all of them were to discover on New Year's Eve.

It was six o'clock in the afternoon. The apartment was quiet. With the door to Remington's room open, Bobby could hear part of the conversation between Remington and his parents and grandparents. It excited him, and he wanted to share the news with his family. Plus, he hoped it would change the minds of some of his cousins and even his brother and sisters. Many of them had told him last night they were unhappy that they never got to leave the tree and that he always got to go everywhere with Remington.

But it was Dazzling who was the most difficult. She had started an argument with Bobby soon after he had been returned to his pod. She griped and griped and said every bulb should get to go see part of the city and visit lots of different places.

He had tried to explain to her and all of his family that Remington believed Bobby had special powers, and he was also impressed that Bobby was able to say his own name in English. *"That's the only reason he chooses me,"* said Bobby. *"Now that I helped get him back with his parents, I guess he'll probably keep taking me places. I can't help it."* Most of his cousins and his brother and two sisters all apologized for being jealous.

But Dazzling never was satisfied and continued to whine that Bobby got to do everything.

"Hey, Dazzling!" It was the third time Flash had yelled at her within the last minute.

"I suppose you have something else to say to insult me," Dazzling shouted back.

"No." Flash chuckled. *"I'm just telling you the truth. Our cousin, Bobby Bright, is the most amazing bulb in the world, and this is just another reason why."* Before Dazzling could answer him, Flash continued, *"Go ahead, Bobby, tell us the story one more time. It's too good to hear only once."*

So Bobby repeated what he had overheard Remington and his family talking about.

"It's going to be like the past two years. We are going to get to shine for another big party, but this time, it will be even better. Remington's classmates from school are coming here to the apartment the day before Christmas.

"There is a big empty room on the third floor," Bobby explained. *"It is right above us and down the hall from Mr. and Mrs. McGillicuddy's room. Mrs. McGillicuddy said it was so big they could hold their big Christmas party inside that one room itself."*

"Oh my goodness," said Bobby's mom. *"That must be a huge room."*

"Yep," Bobby said. *"Remington's parents want the whole evening to be special. They said they wanted to host a party since they will probably not be living here next year."*

"Do you think people will stare at us and make crazy faces like they did the last two years?"

"I guess so, Energizer," Bobby answered his feisty little cousin, who was lying just beneath him near the front of the tree. "One thing for certain; we will have fun, and we will get to sing our very own song again."

"Yeah!"

"That's great news."

"I am so happy."

Lots of *Bulbese* cheers echoed throughout the tree. The bulbs all remembered how special the last two years had been at the McGillicuddys' big Christmas party where they had finally gotten to shine for people and make them happy.

"We'll make everyone here happy, too," Aunt Glaring said as she leaned over and tapped against Bobby.

"But this year it will be even better," added Dimmer. "We'll be the brightest bulbs in the world again, but this time for Remington's friends and all the children in his class."

Suddenly, the cheering was interrupted by something the bulbs couldn't believe they were hearing.

"Bobby, none of this would be possible without you. I know it now. I'm happier and I know we all are because of what you have done for us, and getting to go on this trip and what we get to do." And before anyone could say a word, Dazzling continued. "And you're right too, Dimmer. It will be better because it is Remington's schoolmates."

"Oh my goodness," said Bobby's mom. "That was wonderful, Dazzling."

Bobby leaned over to his mom. "Did she really say that?"

"Yes, Bobby, she did, and maybe we can all learn from this."

"What, Mom?"

"Sometimes it takes longer to be convinced and to change, but if you are good, it can happen. Your cousin, Dazzling, has just shown us she really is a good bulb."

"Thanks, Dazzling," shouted Bobby. "Wow! It's fun having you as a friend."

17

The Tough Part Is Waiting

Bobby had learned about the party for Remington only a couple of days ago, but it seemed more like two weeks. It was like those days in past years when Bobby would count the days until spring-cleaning while buried in the box in the McGillicuddys' front closet. Then after being out of the closet for two days, he would start counting the days until the day after Thanksgiving and the Christmas tree was decorated.

"It is difficult to be patient."

"What did you say, Bobby?"

"Oh, just thinking out loud, Energizer."

"Well, you sound like Mr. McGillicuddy again," said Aunt Glaring. *"You're talking to yourself."*

Bobby's thoughts were interrupted when Remington raced into the room, hurried past the tree, and nearly slid into the bathroom.

"Boy, is he in a hurry," whispered Bobby. *"I wonder what's going on."*

Less than a minute later, Bobby heard the sound of water running in the shower. It was another three minutes before it stopped, and Remington came running into the room. His hair was wet, and he was trying to dry it with a towel as he hurriedly put on some clothes. Before he could finish getting ready, his mom called from the first floor.

"Remington, come down here quickly. The mail just came. Your grandma is opening all of the letters so you can read them."

"I'm coming," he said and grabbed both of his shoes and quickly put them on. Then he scampered out of the room and down the stairs.

"Could you hear what they were saying downstairs, Bobby?"

"Oh, yeah, Twinkle, I heard."

"Well, what was all of the excitement about? What made Remington start squealing?"

"His mom said that every one of his classmates had replied to the invitation to the party and are planning to attend. She said there will be at least sixty children here for the party.'"

Bobby didn't have to say another word. The cheers rang out throughout the branches, and the bulbs all began to practice their little song.

We're gonna shine all Christmas season.
We're gonna shine every night.
We're gonna shine, shine, shine
And be very, very bright

18
The Big One, Spanish Style

The first time the doorbell rang was just before two o'clock in the afternoon. Remington and his mother went to greet the first guests. Within the next fifteen minutes, the chimes of the bell rang at least a dozen times. Finally, there were so many people inside the apartment and so much to do to be sure all the games were being played correctly that Remington's dad posted a message next to the elevator on the first floor.

Just come on up and make yourself at home.
Vengan adentro y bienvenidos.
Diviértanse. Son tanto familia como nuestra familia.

Children were running throughout the house. There were three different games being played, and in Remington's bedroom, Bobby and the other bulbs watched a very popular Spanish game.

Remington's parents had removed the dresser and a chair from the room so there would be space for a six-foot long box. The wooden sides on it were tall enough that the balls were unable to roll or bounce outside the box. Inside there were three marked-off areas. Each child got to roll three hard wooden balls toward the opposite end. Remington was the official scorer, and he spent over an hour keeping track of everyone's point total as they knocked the balls off of scoring sheets and screamed with joy each time they did.

Shortly after the game concluded, and every child had a chance to play, Remington announced the winner of the "Top Player" award. "The winner is," he said and then waited a moment before saying, "*El ganador es...* " He paused one more time.

"Come on, Remington," yelled Aaron, his best friend from school. "Tell us and quit being dramatic." Then all of his third-grade classmates started laughing.

"The winner is Jacobi."

"*No me digas,*" yelled the tiny little Spanish boy.

"No, I'm not kidding," said Remington. "You had ninety-two out of one hundred points."

Then all the kids cheered, and Jacobi, who was the son of one of the Spanish guards at the embassy, saluted Remington and accepted the award. At that moment, the voice of Remington's mom rang out from the top of the stairs on the third floor of the apartment. "Come on, everybody. We have a huge surprise for all of you."

"Let's go," yelled Kyle, another close friend of Remington who was the tallest student at the school.

"Everybody follow Kyle," shouted Chad, Remington's friend who lived in the same apartment building. "We can all see him."

The kids laughed and chattered in English and Spanish as they lined up behind Kyle. More children who had been playing games on the first floor of the apartment came to join them. Soon there was a line stretched from the top of the stairs on the third floor all the way to the bottom of the second-floor stairs. Those at the end were nearly standing in the first floor living room.

Remington was somewhere near the middle of the line just beyond his bedroom door. One of the American girls standing next to him asked, "What's up there?"

"I don't know, Lizzie. My folks have had that door locked since we moved here. Two days ago, they told me it was unlocked but not to go in the room because there was a surprise for the party inside."

"You mean you didn't sneak up there and peek?" asked Elizabeth's twin sister.

"Oh no, Sarah." Remington laughed slightly. "I learned a lesson last year I will never forget."

"What happened? Was it funny?"

"Nope! It wasn't funny. That's for sure."

"He was telling them the story about jumping off the bed and the accident he had last Christmas."

"Did he tell them you were the hero and saved him?"

"No, Energizer, and I didn't save him. You know Mr. McGillicuddy found him on the floor."

"Don't be modest, Robert...uh...I'm sorry. I mean, Bobby," interrupted Dazzling. "You know you were the one who escaped and flew downstairs and caused Rocket to go crazy. If Mr. McGillicuddy had not come inside to find out why the dog was barking, he wouldn't have found poor Remington in time to save him."

"So," said Aunt Glaring, "did he tell the girls about peeking in the closet when he wasn't supposed to and finding the computer?"

"He had just started when the door at the top of the stairs opened and the children started moving into the room."

"Oh my gosh!" gasped Kyle. He was the first to enter the room, and he nearly knocked over two girls standing behind him when he dashed back out and yelled down the stairs, "You won't believe what's in this room!"

Then he dashed inside, and the children behind him began to push and shove. "Calm down! Don't push," yelled Remington's dad. "There's lots of room inside."

"Boy, it must be something great, Remington," Aaron's brother, Andrew, said. "You know Kyle; he hardly ever gets excited about anything."

And then it was Remington's turn to go into the room. "What do you think, little love bug?"

"I can't believe this, Grandma," Remington said. He stared around the room in disbelief. There were ten rows of chairs with a wide space in between each row. All of his classmates and their parents were sitting down. He stood near his mom and dad at the back of the room and listened to music coming from behind a large curtain at the front of the room. "This is the coolest thing that I've ever seen."

There were clowns and live humanlike puppets walking among the crowd, passing out candy and small wrapped gifts for each child. Remington couldn't believe how beautiful all of the costumes were. "Look at that tall robot on the stage," he exclaimed. "He looks like he's going to fall over each time he takes a step."

Just as Remington said that, the orange and yellow robot fell backward and lost his balance. He landed on his back as screams from the children echoed through the room. The screams became noisier when the body of the robot started to fall apart. Large pieces of the tin costume rolled onto the floor.

The music from behind the curtain got louder, and then the curtain began to rise in the air. The crowd looked in disbelief as a pair of human hands slowly emerged from the open side of the robot.

The crowd began to applaud as a dozen musicians started walking up the back stairs of the stage to join the mysterious robot. Each was wearing a bright red pair of pants and a gold and green jacket with fancy buttons stretching from top to bottom. The colors blended perfectly with the gold robot lying partially broken on the stage.

When each musician had reached the main part of the stage, the trumpets, coronets, clarinets, piccolos, and saxophones blended together in a crescendo, and the children began to clap in rhythm to the music. This continued for over a full minute, and then the clapping suddenly stopped. Cries of excitement came from the audience. Gasps of awe echoed through the huge room.

"Look at that!"

"Wow! Do you see what I see?"

"What's happening?"

All eyes were on the stage. There was a reason for all of the questions. From inside the partially broken robot, a small man, who possibly was a midget, crawled free from inside his costume, which matched the colors of the musicians' uniforms. He rolled to the middle of the stage, stood up, and then somersaulted twice before he leaped off the stage. He continued to do body flips and somersaults as he advanced down the aisle splitting the ten rows of chairs.

There was more twisting and turning and rolling and jumping as he worked his way to the back of the room. His maneuvers were followed by loud cheers and clapping as the children, along with the adults who were standing around the walls of the room, watched in awe. The music played in rhythm to each twist and back flip and ended just as the tumbler landed on his feet next to Remington. The crowd applauded. There were shrill, noisy whistles from some of the Spanish men in the audience.

Because most of the children were now standing and looking toward the rear of the room, Remington was one of the first in the audience to see what was happening back on the stage. "Look at that!" he yelled and pointed. As people began to turn around, their eyes opened wide. On stage were two more midget acrobats who had just jumped out of the fallen robot.

The two other acrobats had blinking lights attached to their costumes and were taking turns somersaulting and jumping into the hands of each other. All of this was taking place as the lights in the room were dimmed until the room was nearly dark. The two acrobats continued to fling themselves back and forth across the stage. It was a wonderful sight with the lights blinking rapidly as the midgets twisted through the air.

Then the volume of the music became louder as the speed of the acrobats increased. The faster the back flips, the faster the music. The audience continued to applaud as the back flips, forward flips, and somersaults continued at an amazing pace until the music abruptly stopped. The two acrobats did a final mid-air, twisting maneuver and landed on their feet, standing back to back. They smiled as the crowd cheered.

Then a voice from the loudspeaker in the room boomed: "*Señores y señoras. Por favor. Su atención al fondo de la gran sala.* Ladies and gentlemen. Turn your attention to the back of the room, please."

As people in the audience turned around, Remington could see the faces of many of his classmates, some of whom were yelling, "Look up there!"

Remington, who was standing next to his grandfather, had been so intrigued with the acrobats onstage, he had not seen where the one standing next to him had gone. "Look, Remington!" said Mr. McGillicuddy.

When Remington turned his head toward the ceiling, he saw what everyone in the room was looking at. There was a long cable with a pulley hanging beneath it. Attached to the pulley was a hook. And attached to the hook was the acrobat who had landed next to Remington. His head nearly touched the thirty-foot high ceiling.

The audience gasped as the pulley began to move. The cable suddenly dropped down from the ceiling, and the pulley with the hook attached sped downward toward the stage. The crowd held their breath until suddenly they heard a *snap,* and the hook came loose from the pulley.

The crowd screamed, and the acrobat fell headfirst toward the stage. As he did, he quickly pulled loose the

149

belt from around his waist that had been attached to the hook. He threw the belt and hook toward the back of the room.

Most of the crowd was so busy watching the flying acrobat; they didn't see his two partners still standing back to back on stage. Just as the hook had snapped free, the two on stage spun around, faced each other, and took two steps back. They reached out and clasped their hands together, forming a safety net for their partner. A split second later, he did a mid-air twist and fell on his back into the cradled arms of his comrades.

As the audience went wild and cheered, the two flung their partner upward. He did one more twisting maneuver in mid-air and landed firmly on his feet, standing upright between the two of them. The band began to play another fast-paced tune, and the crowd applauded as the three performers bowed to the audience.

"What do you think, Remington?" His dad walked up on one side of him, and his mom came from the other side and hugged him.

"This is incredible. Where did all these people come from?"

"Remember you said you wanted to go visit Children's Christmas World? Well, with the help of the Spanish and U.S. Embassies we brought them to you. Now they have to finish soon and get back for a big performance tonight."

"Can we go see it?"

"We will, but probably in a couple of days, after Christmas."

"You mean it continues after Christmas?"

"Remember? We talked about it. We said we would save it for Grandpa and Grandma."

"Oh yeah. It goes until January fourth, right? The day before the Three Kings Parade."

"That's right, Remington. Now, let's go meet some of these acrobats and puppet characters before they have to leave."

"Okay, Daddy, but how did all these people get inside without any of us knowing they were here?"

"That's a story I'll tell you about later."

Mr. and Mrs. McGillicuddy were happy about their son's choice for Christmas Eve dinner. It was the second time since they had arrived in Madrid that the family had eaten at the quaint, tiny family restaurant, which was just one block from the apartment at the top of the hill.

"I love this little place," said Mrs. McGillicuddy. "It's just a perfect spot to have dinner before we go to church."

At that moment, the owner and only waiter, Pepe, hurried up to the table. He was tending to all nine tables neatly placed throughout the three tiny rooms of the restaurant that had been in his family for over fifty years.

"*Buenas noches, ustedes.*"

"*Buenas noches y feliz navidad,*" Remington's dad answered.

"Good evening," Mrs. McGillicuddy said softly.

"Go ahead, Grandma," Remington said, "tell Pepe 'good evening' in Spanish."

"Oh, Remington. I can't."

"Well, I can," said Mr. McGillicuddy. "Bueno nokus, Pepe!"

The owner stared at Mr. McGillicuddy with a funny look on his face. Then he smiled and said, "*Buen dicho, señor.*"

Remington was laughing, his parents were laughing, and then Pepe started to laugh.

"Pepe says you said good evening perfectly. But believe me, he's just being nice." Then Remington's dad said to the waiter, "*Eso no es la verdad.*"

And Remington chipped in by affirming what his father had just said. "*Es correcto, Pepe. No es la verdad.*"

Then Pepe laughed, shook Mr. McGillicuddy's hand, and said to Richard, "*¿Dos botellas del agua sin gas?*"

"*Perfecto, y sus tapas favoritas para la mesa también.*"

"*Por seguro, señor.*" Pepe quickly walked away from the table, which was tucked in the corner of the back room of the restaurant.

Mrs. McGillicuddy started to laugh. "Were you laughing about your grandpa, Remington?"

"Yes. The waiter said Grandpa had said good evening perfectly."

"I did?"

"No, Grandpa, you didn't. That's why we were laughing. It sounded like another language the way you said good evening in Spanish."

"Well, I thought I said it just like he did."

Remington's dad started laughing once more. "Not quite, but at least you got the first letter right in both words."

Then everyone but Mr. McGillicuddy laughed in unison.

"What was all that other stuff you were talking about, Richard?" Mrs. McGillicuddy asked.

"Let me tell her, honey," Remington's mom spoke for the first time.

"You know, I told you I am taking some basic Spanish courses. "Let me see if it is helping. I think Richard asked for our favorite appetizer."

"Yes, I did. What else?"

"I'm not sure, but did you tell Pepe that it wasn't correct about what he said about Dad?"

"Yes. I just told him that dad had certainly not said good evening correctly."

"And, of course, you ordered two bottles of water without gas," she continued.

"Good job, Mom! You got it right." Remington then turned and looked at his father. "You promised me back at the party that you would tell me how you got all those people upstairs in that big room without anyone knowing it."

"You know the fire escape at the back of the building?"

"I know," Remington answered. "You told me never to even think about climbing up those stairs and not to play on it."

"That's the one. Well, we sneaked all those people into the patio behind the building just before noon. Then we had a special lunch brought in by the cooks at the embassy. We had gifts that we presented to each of the performers as they were eating.

"By the time they finished, it was time for them to begin putting on all of their makeup and costumes. While they were doing that we had some workers from the embassy bring in some large pieces of sheet rock, and we put those boards up against the patio doors downstairs. We even put signs up that read, 'Obreros adentro.'"

"What does that mean, dear?"

"It means workers inside, Mom. It was just to make sure no one opened the door out of curiosity."

"When people started to arrive, they sat very quietly on the patio until all of the guests had gotten inside. Once the party started, it was easy for them to come up the fire escape and into the ballroom upstairs."

"But, Dad, how did they get all of those wires and all of those platforms and huge figures into the room?"

Before he could answer, Pepe sat a huge plate of various tapas and other appetizers in the middle of the table. "I'll explain the rest while we eat. Okay, everybody, hand me a plate, and let's enjoy these goodies."

"Just tell me what I'm eating first."

"It's all good, Mom."

"I'm sure it is, but tell me."

"Well, there is calamari."

"I know, squid. I never thought I could eat that until I tried it earlier this week. It was delicious."

"And," Remington's dad continued, "we have blood sausage, regular sausage, meatballs, the crab sandwiches, and even some snails if you want to get brave. And there's more."

"I'm brave," said Mr. McGillicuddy. "Let me have one of each."

19

Christmas Morning Confessions

Mr. and Mrs. McGillicuddy slowly walked up the stairs from the first floor holding hands. "John, I am worn out. It's three o'clock in the morning."

"I know, dear," Mr. McGillicuddy said and gently squeezed the hands of his wife. "This is the most amazing Christmas Eve we've ever had in our lives. There will never be another one like it. That cathedral was absolutely beautiful. Just think of it; the bishop of Madrid was there. He is one of the highest-ranking members of the church in Spain."

"And what was amazing to me," Mrs. McGillicuddy interrupted him, "was the fact that even though I couldn't understand one word, I still felt as though I knew exactly what was happening.

"It was so wonderful when the people inside the cathedral all lined up to go to the altar and offer something to the nativity scene."

"Well, the fact we were in a mammoth cathedral built over six hundred years ago certainly made it even more special." He started to say something else, but Mrs. McGillicuddy grabbed his arm and said, "Shhh!"

They stopped outside Remington's bedroom door. "What is that noise? Did you hear it?"

Mr. McGillicuddy grinned and said, "Oh, yes, dear. I heard it. And I bet I know what it is." He quickly grabbed the handle and flung the door open.

"John, what are you doing? Be quiet! You will wake Remington."

"No, I won't. He's sound asleep. See." He pointed to the bed where Remington's head could barely be seen beneath two large blankets laying atop him.

"And you little guys won't wake him either." Then he bent down, and as Mrs. McGillicuddy watched in disbelief, he stuck his face right up against the bulbs at the front of the tree. "I know all about you miracle bulbs. And I know you are special. So don't think for a moment I don't know what all of you can do."

"John McGillicuddy." She grabbed him by the arm and pulled him away from the tree. "Have you lost your mind?"

"No, but I know these bulbs made the noise and they are magical. When Remington was lost in that huge crowd, we knew there was little chance to find him. Then suddenly there he is, safe and unharmed.

"Then just as we are about to find out what happens, along comes this homeless woman with a story of a flying bulb, which we, of course, all laugh about. But maybe we shouldn't laugh anymore."

Mrs. McGillicuddy started to say something, but he didn't give her time. "You know why? It's because maybe that blue bulb right there in the front of the tree did save him."

"You have had too much excitement tonight. You definitely need to get some sleep."

He didn't answer her. He just put his right hand in her left hand and held it firmly. She looked at her husband. "John, tell me exactly why you believe all of this."

"Okay," he answered, "but don't laugh at me."

Mrs. McGillicuddy stared into the darkness. There was some light from the street four floors below. It sneaked through the nearly closed blinds of the balcony door. She turned her head and saw the clock on the bed stand.

The time was 4:30. She had been trying to fall asleep for the last hour. It wasn't easy with Mr. McGillicuddy snoring loudly. He never had trouble going to sleep.

"How can he believe that blue bulb really can do all those things?" she whispered to herself. "I love John, but sometimes he worries me. I know he's not losing his mind, but he sure says goofy things. And yet, I'm about to believe him anyway."

Then she rolled over and put the pillow over her head for a moment. She lay there for only a few seconds, and when she took the pillow away and rolled over onto her back, she looked again at the clock. It read 4:31 a.m.

"Nope," she said softly to herself. "I'm not dreaming. I'm beginning to believe, too. There is something strange going on. I'm going to have a talk with Remington tomorrow." Then she yawned and stretched her arms. "But right now, I've got to get some sleep. It's Christmas. We've got a big day ahead of us."

"You look tired, Mom."

"Well, I didn't sleep very well, Lisa."

"You look okay to me, Grandma. Merry Christmas."

"I hope I always look good to you, Remington," Mrs. McGillicuddy said. "But I can't stay awake until five o'clock in the morning and then get up at ten and expect to feel real good."

"Five o'clock? You didn't go to bed until then? What did you and Dad do?" Lisa asked.

"Well, he didn't do anything but sleep once we got to bed at around 3:15. We talked in the kitchen after all of you went to bed at 2:30. Then we stood on the balcony outside our room for a while. We enjoyed looking at all of those Santa Clauses hanging on the ropes outside the buildings along *Fomento*. That is such a neat custom.

"And then we started upstairs to bed. However, we stopped in your room for a couple of minutes, Remington. That's when it all began."

Remington's mom was busy making pancakes and didn't realize Mrs. McGillicuddy had stopped talking until she suddenly looked up and saw her mother-in-law staring into space. "Mom, are you okay?"

"Yeah, Grandma. Are you okay? You are acting funny."

"Well, your grandfather has got me thinking about some strange things."

"What are you talking about?" asked Lisa.

"Remington, you continue to swear that this bulb you call Bobby really did guide you back to that department store. It's too much to want to believe, and yet too many things have happened for me to not think it is possible."

"It's just outrageous to talk this way," said Lisa.

"No it's not, Mom, if it's the truth."

"What's outrageous?" asked Remington's dad as he walked in the room. "By the way, *feliz navidad, mi familia.*"

"Merry Christmas, Daddy," Remington said and raced into his arms and gave him a big hug.

"Where's your Grandpa?"

"Did somebody mention my name?" Mr. McGillicuddy asked as he walked into the kitchen.

"Yes, we've been talking about you because of what you told me last night."

"Oh," Mr. McGillicuddy said sheepishly. He tucked his head and looked down at the floor. A moment later he looked up. "You mean, you told them?"

"Yes, and I want you to tell all of them what you believe right now."

"Well, okay. I might as well tell you everything. It seems Christmas is the perfect day to talk about amazing Christmas tree light bulbs."

"I've known that for two years," said Remington.

"Let your grandfather fill us in on the mystery," Remington's dad said and then laughed.

"Maybe you won't laugh after I tell you all of the things that have happened."

What followed from the lips of Mr. McGillicuddy made Christmas in Spain even more special, and the bulbs on Remington's tree even more mysterious.

He admitted to lots of strange things happening. They included hearing noises from the bulbs on the tree in Remington's room, both in America and in Madrid; how two broken bulbs last year were found on the tree in Remington's room at the McGillicuddys house after they had been unscrewed and removed by Mrs. McGillicuddy; how he had seen the tree branches shake on Remington's tree, both back home and here in Madrid; how he was certain he had seen something looking like a bulb fly up the stairs just before he found Remington injured in his room the day before Christmas last year.

And the two biggest stories included believing the bulbs had saved Mrs. McGillicuddy from bleeding to death during the tornado a year ago and the old homeless woman here in Madrid who claimed a flying bulb had saved Remington.

When he had finished, Remington added, "And don't forget that blue bulb, Bobby, can say his own name."

20
Bobby Tells the Good News

It was 10:30 in the evening. Everyone was exhausted from a Christmas day that had been marvelous. They had opened presents (except for Remington, who would open his presents on January 6 like the other children in Spain) and enjoyed *roscón de reyes,* a traditional Spanish pastry with a surprise toy inside that made you a very important person if it was found inside your slice of cake. Mr. and Mrs. McGillicuddy had gone to bed an hour earlier because they were so tired after having slept only a few hours on Christmas Eve. Remington was asleep on the living room sofa.

Remington's parents were sitting at the kitchen table talking about the wonderful Christmas all of them had enjoyed when Remington's dad said, "Let's go upstairs to Remington's room. I want to check something on the tree. I'll explain when we get there." He stood up and quickly walked into the hallway.

"Wait a minute! Take Remington up to his room."

"Okay." He walked to the sofa, lifted him up, and trudged up the stairs.

She followed him, and once Remington was tucked under the covers of his bed, he turned to her and said, "You know something, I actually believed Dad when he was telling those stories."

"I've heard enough of this!"

"Well, some of those things are hard to dispute."

"Richard, please! Surely you don't think that bulb really flew through the air and saved Remington when he got lost. And surely you don't believe the bulb can say Bobby?"

"Just listen to me." He pulled loose from her and started to turn on the light switch.

"Don't do that," she said. "You'll wake him up."

"All right, but I need to check something on that strand. You know, Lisa, of all people, you should believe some of those stories. Remember after Christmas last year at Mom and Dad's? At the time, I thought you were either having bad dreams or a bit crazy. And for sure, I thought you were seeing things. I mean, you are the one who told me about the tree limbs shaking and the bulbs bouncing on Remington's tree. So maybe you saw something too."

"Oh, honey, please!"

"Well, regardless, watch."

"What are you going to do?"

"I want to look at those bulbs for a moment and check the plugs. I've decided to surprise Remington with a very special Christmas gift that will cost practically nothing and should be a lot of fun."

"What?"

"Well, we know he's been taking that blue bulb off the tree and carrying it with him wherever we go. And I've caught him a couple of times holding it up in the air and pointing at things as if he were actually showing the bulb something. Plus, he's talked to the bulb on a number of occasions, even though he tries not to be seen."

"Well, darling," she nudged him with her elbow and smiled, "it's probably good because it's like having our own bodyguard for Remington."

"Yeah, maybe you are right," he chuckled. "Anyway, what's important is he believes all of these bulbs are special. So here's the idea I had, and I've already seen it will work. There is this guy at the embassy. He is a technical genius. A week ago he was showing me a small container that produces light and energy and allows you to carry light bulbs with you to use when needed.

"So I had this idea. We can take one of those small little boxes and put them in a bag. Then we plug the strand of bulbs into it. Next, we wrap the bulbs around Remington's shoulders and neck. Maybe we even put some of the strand around his forehead. We light him up. It would be so funny for the New Year's Eve celebration at *Puerta del Sol*. It's supposed to be wild and crazy. You know how much the folks laughed last week when we went walking down *Calle de Preciados*, and people were everywhere with those crazy wigs. Well, I hear there are thousands of people wearing those wigs on New Year's Eve. It will be fun. Remington can be our own walking Christmas tree with all the lights around him."

He bent down to check the plug in the wall socket, and before he could say anything else, he heard his wife laugh. He looked up at her. "What?"

"You're right dear. With tens of thousands of people in *Puerta Del* Sol on New Years Eve, if we get lost, at least Bobby can help us find our way home."

Then they both broke into laughter.

Remington's bedroom was much darker than the room he stayed in at his grandparents' house in America. Sliding, pull-down blinds in front of balcony windows were popular in Spain, and blocked outside light. However, there was one blind on the far right side of the room that didn't work correctly. A sliver of light from the street lamp below the second floor balcony managed to sneak its way into the room. It was enough for Bobby to see Remington lying in bed.

Christmas day had turned out to be colder than normal for Madrid. Remington's mom had put another blanket over him before he fell asleep. His head could barely be seen, sticking out from under the thick bedspread.

Bobby still couldn't believe what Remington's parents had been talking about. He wanted to tell all of the bulbs right now.

"This is really special and strange, too, because our gift to humans is shining and making people happy. We aren't supposed to receive gifts. Here I am again, sounding like Mr. McGillicuddy, talking to myself."

"Wake up! All of you wake up! I have something to tell you, even though you may not believe it."

Aunt Glaring yawned and twisted herself so she could see him. "What's happening?"

Before he could answer, his mom and sisters all said in unison, "What's going on? Why are you yelling? I'm trying to sleep."

There were more cries.

"Is it morning?"

"What's going on?"

Bobby answered, "Don't panic. Just listen. I have something important to tell you."

When Bobby finished explaining what he overheard, there were plenty of questions to answer.

"You mean Mr. McGillicuddy actually told them about your dad and Whitening disappearing and then returning?"

"Oh, yeah, Uncle Flicker. He told them that story and especially about the tornado and Mrs. McGillicuddy. He kept repeating over and over that he knew for certain it was us who had saved her."

"Well, it's amazing," said Bobby's mom. "I have to admit, Bobby Bright, that you have angered me, been ornery and feisty, and done things you shouldn't have done. However, it appears now those things may have been a blessing."

Bobby started to say something, but his mom shook herself at him. "No, let me finish. It's almost like we have become part of the McGillicuddy family. Remington and Mr. McGillicuddy know for certain that you are the most special bulb.

"Remington likes to steal you away from the tree and take you different places. He knows you are the most magical."

Bobby raised his voice so all could hear. "I'm repeating what I've said many times. We are all special, and because of that I've saved the best news until last, and it will prove we all deserve the best." He waited a moment to be sure every bulb was listening. "Remington's dad is planning a surprise for him for New Year's Eve, and we are going to be a part of it."

And then Bobby Bright told them about the exciting trip coming up on December 31.

21

A Royal Visit

It was an amazing whirlwind tour of Madrid. Each day something new happened, and each day Bobby came back home in the pocket of Remington with more stories for his family. Even Flash, who had decided Dazzling was right, quit being jealous and listened.

On the twenty-sixth, everyone had rested up from what had been a very tiring past two days. On the twenty-seventh, the fun began. Remington's dad, who had gotten permission from the embassy to not work that week, served as the tour guide.

The first of five straight days of fun started with an open-air bus tour. It had been very, very cold on Christmas Eve and Christmas Day, but the McGillicuddys were lucky. It warmed up, and it was only slightly chilly during the trip through Madrid.

"We went throughout the city," explained Bobby. *"We stopped at lots of different places, and it gave Mr. and Mrs. McGillicuddy the chance to choose the ones to come back to and visit in the next few days. Remington and his parents had seen most of the places but not all of them.*

"We stopped outside the king's palace and walked around in the big area in front. We are going back there tomorrow, I think. It is huge. Think of this," Bobby said. "If you took the house where the McGillicuddys live, you could put two hundred fifty of those houses inside the palace and still have room."

"No way," screamed Twinkle.

"I just know that's what Remington said."

"Yeah, but you know Remington," Sparkle joined her sister in the conversation. "He exaggerates when he is telling you stories, Bobby."

"I know, but his dad laughed when Remington said it and told him they could probably put close to five hundred inside the palace and the grounds around it."

"What else, Bobby?"

"Are you enjoying this, Dad?"

"You bet I am. I'm feeling better than I have in years."

"I'm glad you are happy. You want to hear more?"

"Of course. Go on."

"Before the day was over, we drove past the largest cathedral in Madrid and one of the largest in the country. We visited the opera building, and we passed under some amazing tall towers, which is where the signals and the power comes for radio and television stations. We also went to the bullfighting ring."

"What's that?"

"You, of all bulbs, should know that answer, Uncle Flicker."

"Yeah, Dad," Blinker said. "Remember. It was about four years ago, and you said you saw some pictures on the television screen when we were on the back of the big tree downstairs. You said it was bullfighting and all the bullfighters looked funny in their tight pants and jackets. You said they were carrying blankets."

"Capes," Bobby interrupted. "They are called capes."

"You know, I do remember now," said Flicker. "They have four legs, and those things on their heads are called horns, right?"

"You got it," said Bobby. "We are going to see the bullfights Sunday."

"I want to see a bullfight, too, Bobby."

"Be quiet, Blinker," Flicker scolded his son. "You know you can't go see those fights. Go on, Bobby. Tell us about the rest of the tour today."

And Bobby did, telling them about the trip along *Gran Via*, seeing the cable cars going up the tall hills on the edge of Madrid, and about the huge park called *El Retiro*, where almost every family that ever lived in Madrid has walked and played in. He told them of seeing the huge *El Prado* museum. He told them about the huge plazas and fountains and buildings dating back to the sixteenth century. And he also told them of passing the *Atocha* train station where the terrible terrorist bombings had happened several years ago.

"It sounds like it took all day, Bobby."

"No, but it did last six hours. But it was so much fun; it didn't seem that long. Of course, I didn't understand very much about what we saw."

"Why, because you don't speak Spanish?"

Bobby laughed and answered, "Real funny, Energizer. The whole tour was narrated in English and Spanish."

"So what happens tomorrow?"

"Like I said, Aunt Glaring, I think we are going to the royal palace."

"Well, I'll bet there will be plenty to tell us after that visit."

"Remington's dad was right. You could put five hundred houses the size of the McGillicuddys' house inside that palace."

"How could any place be that big?"

"I don't know, Mom, but I heard Mr. McGillicuddy say that after it burned down, it took over fifteen years to build."

"Fifteen years to build a house. Boy, those folks didn't know how to work."

"Uncle Flicker, you are so funny at times." Bobby laughed. "This was over three hundred fifty years ago. It was the eighteenth century, and actually the palace goes all the way back to the tenth century. This is not the original one. It was built in the sixteenth century and burned down a hundred years later."

"How can you remember all of this, Bobby? You really are smart."

"Not really, Dazzling. That's about all I remember, except the rooms are huge, and the furniture is large, and beautiful."

"Quiet, Bobby," Aunt Glaring interrupted. "I hear the McGillicuddys."

"If we don't visit another place or see anything else, today made the trip worth while," Mr. McGillicuddy said as he and Remington walked into the bedroom.

"I told you. Mom and Dad and I wanted to take you there. We saw it once, but it was still like seeing it for the first time because it is so large and there is so much to see."

"Well, it was a wonderful tour, and I will never forget the size of the rooms and how beautiful the furniture is. The art work is unbelievable, although I can't stand most of it."

"Why?"

"Oh, you know. All those fancy kings and queens and all those crazy weird paintings with half animals and man. I just don't understand it."

Remington laughed. "You know, I'm only nine years old, but I understand. Those are masterpieces. Unbelievable art."

"Didn't say they weren't." Mr. McGillicuddy chuckled. "Just said they aren't my cup of tea."

"Your cup of tea? What's that supposed to mean?"

"Nothing." Mr. McGillicuddy smiled. "It just means I'm not a connoisseur of fine art."

"What's conno...conno...?"

"Connoisseur." Mr. McGillicuddy repeated. "Oh, it means I'm not smart enough to understand what's supposed to be good."

"You're kidding, right?"

"Only a little bit." Mr. McGillicuddy laughed again. "Now, go! We can talk while you put your pajamas on."

Remington walked into his closet and found his pajamas. He started getting undressed. A moment later he returned into the room with his new pajamas on. His grandfather asked him, "You know what I had the most fun at today?"

"What, Grandpa?"

"I enjoyed the royal armory the most. That museum was unbelievable."

"I liked it too," Remington said. "I liked all those swords and old guns, and my favorite thing was all the different armor that the knights wore. It's amazing how it changed throughout the centuries."

"I'll never know how those soldiers could even walk, let alone ride a horse, with all that armor on."

"Hey, what's going on here? Is this a flashback to another great day together?" Remington's dad said as he walked into the room.

"It was wonderful, Richard. I still can't believe we saw only fifty rooms on that tour. It took nearly three hours. Can you imagine how long it would take to see all 2,800 rooms?"

"It is quite a sight. I heard you talking about the armory when I walked in. I agree. Those knights of armor were something special. And all those horses with all the armor wrapped around their bodies. I don't even know how they could move."

"Well, it was interesting and educational, and something to always remember," Mr. McGillicuddy added, and then he pulled the bed covers up to Remington's chin and reached down and gave him a kiss.

"Glad you had a great time, Grandpa. We did too, didn't we, Daddy?"

"Better than that. We had a super time. Now get a good night's sleep because tomorrow is our trip to see the bullfights."

22
A Surprise Trip for Blinker

"**T**hanks for telling us about the palace trip. It must have been fun."

"It was something else, Mom. All five of them spent over two hours in the garden behind the palace. Remington's dad said they must have walked twenty blocks by the time they left the palace."

"What are blocks again?" Sparkle asked.

"It's the distance between streets."

"Oh," she said, but Bobby knew she didn't understand.

"Bobby, I love you," said Aunt Glaring, "but I am tired just from listening to all the stories. Can we go to sleep?"

"Go to sleep everyone. More stories coming tomorrow. It's time for the bullfights."

"You are so lucky," shouted Blinker. "I still wish I could see them."

"Go to sleep, Blinker. I told you that's impossible," Flicker said.

At the other end of the strand, Bobby whispered to his mom, "If only Uncle Flicker knew. Have I got a surprise for him and Blinker."

Remington's hair was still wet from his early morning shower. His mom grabbed the towel lying on the bed and threw it over his head. "Hurry up! Dry your hair. We just have time to eat some breakfast before we walk to the church. Grandma will want to take extra time and stroll through the garden at the rear of the palace. She has fallen in love with how pretty it is, so it will take us longer than usual."

Remington rubbed his head with the towel and then lifted it in the air in dramatic fashion before dropping it to the floor. He stretched his arms to both sides with the palms of his hands upward. "Voila! The hair is completely dry. What do you think?"

"Okay, Mr. Redheaded Magician. It looks fine. Now, come on."

"Mom, are we going right to the bullfight after church?"

"No, first we are going to go to *La Quintana* for a quick lunch. You can introduce your grandparents to your favorite waiter, Mariano. Then we will take the metro to Las Ventas."

"*Ventas?* What's that? I thought that meant sales or for sale."

"No, honey, that's the name of the plaza del toros, the stadium for the bull fights. So come on." She took his hand. "Let's get downstairs."

Remington jerked his hand free. "Not yet," he said. "I have to get Bobby."

"Oh, Remington, are you taking that bulb again?"

Then, she quickly smiled. "Okay. Take him, but come downstairs right now. You can get him when you come back to brush your teeth."

Bobby waited until Remington and his mom were downstairs. Then he said in a loud voice so all could hear, *"Blinker, you are in for a big surprise."*

"What do you mean?" yelled Blinker.

"Bobby, what are you planning to do?"

Bobby whispered, *"Don't panic, Mom. I'm going to take Blinker with me today."* Then he yelled, *"I've got a surprise for you Blinker. You and Uncle Flicker and Aunt Shining sometimes get left out, being at the other end of the strand. You don't get to hear all the conversation up here.*

"So," Bobby continued, *"I am going to see if you can go to the bullfight, Blinker."*

"What are you talking about?" Uncle Flicker growled.

"Let me explain."

"Bobby Bright, you listen to me," said Aunt Shining. *"That sounds scary. I'm not sure I want Blinker to leave here. But more importantly, just how do you think you can*

get him out of his pod, and why do you think Remington will decide to take another bulb with him?"

"Just wait and see," said Bobby and then he uttered "Puhrumba! Puhrumba!"

Aunt Shining looked through the thin branches. She was amazed again at the things her nephew could do. There he was hovering in the air and looking down at the tree. "It's just like last year when he saved his father and Whitening," she said to Flicker.

"I know, dear; the boy is something special."

"Is he really going to do this, Dad?" Blinker asked Flicker.

"I think so, Son. He's got his mind made up."

"Here I go," shouted Bobby from above, and then as Blinker looked into the air, he felt a sudden shock inside him, and he began spinning inside his pod.

"Wow! This is fun…I think." He gulped. Now he was spinning faster, and then seconds later, he popped loose. The pressure from the rush of air lifted him slightly into the air, only inches from the pod.

"Oh, Bobby," screamed Aunt Shining. "What are you doing to my son?"

Bobby looked down with a smile on his face, and he quickly reduced his midair spin while hovering above Flicker, Shining, and Blinker. "Just setting him free, Aunt Shining; he'll be okay."

"You be careful with me."

"Hang on, Blinker," Bobby answered back. "Just have fun." Then Bobby rotated as hard as he could, and the current of air sucked Blinker away from the branch. Quickly he was in the air, moving sideways, and in just three seconds, Bobby managed to get him situated on another branch at the front of the tree.

"There you are, cousin," Bobby said as he glided down and landed beside Blinker, who was now laying partially on the cord between Aunt Glaring and Bobby.

Bobby's mom leaned forward and smiled. "Blinker, is that really you?"

Blinker started to answer but was interrupted by the voice of Twinkle. "I wish I could go," she said.

"Me too, Bobby," said Sparkle.

"Come on, sisters, give me a break. You know Remington isn't going to take every bulb."

"We know. Just wishing," said Twinkle.

"I'm wishing too, but I understand," added Dimmer.

From other parts of the tree came more cries.

"Don't worry, Bobby."

"It's okay, Bobby."

"We understand, Bobby."

When the excitement and the rat-a-tat-tat sound of Bulbese quieted, Bobby's mom asked Blinker, "Do you really want to do this?"

"Oh, yeah," he answered. "This is exciting."

Bobby leaned sideways and clinked his body against Blinker. He smiled and said, "*Let's hope the rest of the day is even more exciting.*"

23

Olé!

"This is exciting, although I'm not sure I'm going to like what they do to those bulls," Mrs. McGillicuddy said.

"*¡Olé! Olé!*" The cries came from throughout the stadium.

Remington stood up with a bulb in each hand. "See," he shouted to Bobby, "this is amazing."

Then a trumpet sounded, and the crowd began to quiet. Everyone's attention turned to one of the long tunnels that stretched from beneath the stadium to the arena floor. The crowd remained standing and began singing in unison. Within a few seconds, the spectators began to applaud. Then the singing turned to loud whistles, mostly coming from the men in the audience.

As the McGillicuddy family looked down into the Plaza del Toros, the noise became even louder as five men in two separate lines, each dressed in dark red jackets and tight-fitting gold pants, walked side by side into the arena. Behind them were two men on horseback. They were dressed in silver pants and high-top boots that were decorated with silver and gold. Each rider had on a wide-brimmed hat. They were not sombreros but smaller hats that were still large enough to block out the sunlight, which was very bright for a December afternoon.

"You know, this is only the second bullfight we have been to, and we probably won't go again. We just wanted you to see one. And this is very rare. Normally they don't have bullfights in Madrid in December, but this is part of a special festival that is celebrated every few years."

"What kind of festival?" Mrs. McGillicuddy asked her son.

"I'm not sure of all the details, but it has to do with some ancient traditions that are celebrated just once every decade. And there is no question, bullfighting, like it or not, is a tradition in Spain."

At that time, the trumpets blared even louder from the arena floor, and the crowd stood and cheered as the last three men in the procession entered the arena. They were the *matadors* or *toreros,* the men who would fight the bulls.

Each wore a jacket that was a mixture of red, gold, blue, and green colors and were covered with beads and sequins. Now they passed by the men on horseback and the other brightly clad *banderilleros* and continued to the center of the arena where they hoisted their hats into the air and waved to the crowd. Then they turned and, with long strides, marched side by side directly to the middle of one side of the bowl-shaped arena. Hanging from the wall in front of an area filled with high-backed velvet chairs was a large drapery with the colors of Spain on it. It wasn't the national flag, but it looked very much like one. A man stood up and the crowd cheered.

"What's going on, Richard?" Mr. McGillicuddy asked.

"The three matadors are presenting themselves to the chief dignitary for today's performance. I think I read in the paper the *alcalde* of Madrid would be here."

"That means the mayor of Madrid," Lisa said to Mrs. McGillicuddy.

"Boy, Mom, that's good," interrupted Remington. "You are getting better at Spanish.

"Yes, very impressive," said Mrs. McGillicuddy.

"All right, we can sit down," said Remington's dad. "The show is about to begin."

Remington was sitting next to his grandmother, and he tugged at Mrs. McGillicuddy's hand. "Grandma, see the men on horseback?" The two who had led the procession now turned their horses in opposite directions. One went to an exit tunnel and the other proceeded to the middle of the ring.

"Yes. What are those pads that are wrapped around the body and the legs of those horses they are riding?"

"That's what I was getting ready to tell you. Those are to protect them from the horns of the bull."

"Ohhhh!" Mrs. McGillicuddy shivered and shook her head. "Why? What's going to happen?"

"Well, the man on horseback is going to bring this long sword out..."

Before Remington could continue, his dad interrupted him. "Actually, it's not a sword; it's called a lance. It's like a spear. There,"—he pointed toward the man on horseback—"It is about nine to ten feet long. This is part one of three stages of the fight and where the bull begins to get worn down."

At that moment, the crowd roared, and the first of the six bulls that would be fought charged into the ring. The *picadaor* shifted forward in the saddle and took a stronger grip on the lance, which was leaning against the right side of the padded horse.

The McGillicuddys had a perfect view. They had been fortunate because even though they weren't able to sit in the lower part of the arena, they had gotten seats on the very first row of the upper level. There was no one in front of them to block their view.

More wild cheers echoed throughout *Las Ventas*. The bull charged toward the horse and then slid to a stop and pawed the ground. The *picador* nudged his boots against the sides of the giant animal, and it lumbered forward slowly. The weight of the heavy pads prevented the horse from moving fast. After only a few feet, the *picador* pulled on the reins, and the horse immediately stopped.

The bull charged and rammed his horns hard into the pads. At that moment, the *picador* raised the lance into the air and plunged the point of the blade into the neck of the bull. It was a clean entrance, and the crowd cheered. Then the *picador* pulled the lance free and backed the horse away as the bull stuck his nose into the dirt, backed up, and pawed again as if he were ready to charge.

It was at that moment the cheers of the crowd increased as the eyes of nearly everyone in the stands focused on one of the protective narrow wooden walls that sat just a few feet from the arena wall. From behind the *burladero* marched the first of the three matadors. He confidently walked toward the bull and the horse and rider. He held a large red cape to his side as he strode with confidence toward the middle of the arena. He approached the bull, which was continuing to paw at the ground in front of the horse, and to get the bull's attention, the matador made an upward movement of his left hand into the air. He then followed with a sweeping move of the red cape, placing it only two feet away from the bull's face. The bull charged immediately. In dramatic fashion, the matador swept the cape over the head and back of the bull as it raced past him. Then the matador turned his back on the animal and walked away.

It was the *picador's* turn once again. He prompted the horse to move forward. As he did, the bull charged, and the *picador* raised the long lance as high as he could and managed to plunge it into the middle of the bull's back. It was a clean, quick maneuver. The crowd again cheered loudly.

"Ohhh!" It was Mrs. McGillicuddy. "That's awful!"

"Grandma. Just watch. This is part of the fight. It's traditional."

"All right, but I'm not sure I'm going to like this."

"This is the time when the *matador* studies the bull for any different techniques or moves he might make. The bull is starting to feel weaker."

"Well, it's not fair to the bull, Richard," Mrs. McGillicuddy quivered.

"I know. I'm just explaining."

"Look, Bobby!" Remington held both bulbs up in the air and leaned over the railing. "See?"

"Be careful, Remington," sternly shouted his mom above the noise. "That railing is short. You could fall if you lean too far. And put those bulbs away before you drop one."

Remington stepped back from the railing but continued to hold the bulbs in the air.

"It was absolutely amazing," said Blinker.

"Hey, Bobby! You shouldn't have taken Blinker to the bullfights. You may never get to talk again."

The bulbs all laughed and Bobby said, *"You are right, Flash. This is more than Blinker has spoken in his entire life."*

"Well, it was exciting," said Blinker. "But you go ahead, Bobby, and finish. You are better at this than I am."

"I still remember Mrs. McGillicuddy after the banderilleros had entered the ring. Remington's dad explained that they were the men who really wore the bull down and made him weaker for the torero. There were two of them, and they would alternate, daringly jumping in front of the bull."

"Oh my gosh! You mean they stood in front of a bull running toward them?"

"Oh, yes, Aunt Glaring," Bobby answered. "At the last moment they would jump to the side and attempt to plunge one of those banderillas into the back or the neck of the bull. When they had each put three into it, the bull was much, much weaker. Then the matador stepped forward and began the final fight. It was then Mrs. McGillicuddy said, 'I think I am going to faint.'"

"But she didn't, did she?" Bobby's mom asked anxiously.

"No, but she covered her eyes a lot in the next few minutes."

Bobby paused as if he was trying to remember, and then Uncle Flicker bellowed again from the lower branches. "Well, don't keep us in suspense. What else happened?"

"Give him time, Dad," said Blinker, who was back in his pod next to his mom.

"Well, I remember Mr. McGillicuddy got more excited than anyone, and then he told Mrs. McGillicuddy, 'I hope you can hold up through all of this, dear.' That was when

189

Remington's dad told them they wouldn't be staying to see all six bulls. He said, 'Three is enough' and told them that this was an event where you could always say you saw one but never wanted to see another one again."

"So tell us, Bobby! I'm tired of waiting. Tell us what happened to the bullfighter."

"Okay, Mom. It's just that apparently those things don't happen very often."

"Well, tell them," said Blinker, "or I will. Quit being so dramatic."

"You'll have to wait, everyone. Ssshh! I hear Remington coming down the hall."

Remington and Mr. McGillicuddy walked into the bedroom. "What did you want to tell me, Remington?"

"You know how you have been talking about all of the strange things that have happened with this strand of Christmas tree lights?"

"Yes."

"Do you believe me when I say I heard the blue bulb say 'Bobby,' and do you believe what happened when I was lost?"

"I believe you if you say it's true." Mr. McGillicuddy cleared his throat. "It's like I said the other day; I am ready to believe almost anything with these bulbs."

"I promise you, Grandpa, I've heard him say what sounded like Bobby at least three times."

"Okay, but what does this do with us having a secret talk?"

"I walked into the bedroom after breakfast this morning. I got my jacket from the closet, and I went to the front of the tree right over there." Remington pointed to the front branches. "You see, Bobby, the blue bulb in front, right?" Remington looked up at his grandfather who was nodding his head. "Well, I started unscrewing Bobby, and just as I was taking him out of the socket, I saw another bulb lying right next to him on the branch. It was weird. I didn't know how it got there. I started to leave it and go, but I decided to look and see if there was a socket empty. I looked at the front and the sides and didn't find any open sockets. Then just as I was about to believe that something else crazy was happening, I looked underneath that branch." Remington pointed across the room to one of the lower branches near the front of the tree. "And there it was."

Remington walked across the room to the tree. He bent down and pulled one of the lower branches up. "Come here, Grandpa." He held the branch up until Mr. McGillicuddy took a few steps across the room and bent down. "Look! See that extension cord that runs from the wall onto the tree? Do you see where the end of the strand is plugged into it?"

"Yes. I can see it."

"Well, it's that green bulb right there." He pointed to the third bulb from the end of the strand. "That's the bulb I put back into its socket. That was the one I had with me at the bullfight along with Bobby."

"So what are you saying? That during the night this bulb escaped from this socket or pod and managed to move up on the tree next to your blue bulb, Bobby?" Before Remington could answer, Mr. McGillicuddy laughed and continued, "See, now you know how I felt these past two years when all these strange things happened. When you first found it, why didn't you either leave it or put it back where it belonged?"

"That's the rest of the story. I had just laid Bobby down on the floor and was getting ready to screw the other bulb in the socket when, and this is the reason I wanted to tell you this alone..." Remington paused and looked at his grandfather.

"What? Quit being dramatic. Tell me what happened."

"I was getting ready to screw the other bulb in, and I heard a clanking sound. I looked and there he was, Bobby, rolling along the floor. I almost dropped the other bulb."

"Why?"

"Why? Did you not hear what I said? Bobby was rolling by itself along the floor."

"Oh my gosh! What did you do?"

"I stopped what I was doing and stood up. When I did, Bobby stopped rolling. I thought I was seeing things, so I

bent down again and started to screw the green bulb in."
Then Remington again quit talking and stared once more
at his grandfather.

Mr. McGillicuddy waited a few seconds and finally said,
"What's wrong?"

"Don't think I'm crazy, Grandpa."

"Don't worry," said Mr. McGillicuddy. "I'm past thinking anyone is crazy when it comes to these bulbs. Tell me,
but it will be our secret."

"Thanks. I started to screw the bulb in the socket,
and I heard the noise again, and this time Bobby was
rolling back toward me. As soon as I stood up again, he
stopped rolling."

Mr. McGillicuddy chuckled. "I think I would have run
out of the room."

"I almost did, but then I figured it out."

"What do you mean you figured it out?"

"I shook my head like I couldn't believe what I was
seeing. I made myself think I hadn't seen Bobby rolling back and forth. I bent down for a third time to try
and screw in the green bulb. It happened again." This
time Remington waited, as if he were enjoying keeping
his grandfather in doubt.

"What happened?"

"Bobby again started rolling away from me on the
floor. Just like that, Grandpa, all by himself. And then I
figured it out. It made sense."

"Nothing about this makes sense."

"No, it does now. Suddenly I understood. You see,"— Remington held his hands out in front of him with palms upward, a smile on his face, and he made one of his eyebrows twitch. He snapped his finger and thumb, but there was hardly any kind of a noise—"just like that, I figured it out. Bobby wanted me to take the other bulb with us to the bullfights. He was trying to tell me to follow him. As soon as I put it in my pocket, Bobby stopped rolling. So I reached down, picked him up, and away we went."

Mr. McGillicuddy stood there with his mouth open staring at Remington. "You're kidding me."

"Nope, I'm not kidding."

"Who's not kidding?"

"Oh my gosh!" yelped Mr. McGillicuddy. He sounded like a dog that had just had his tail stepped on. "You scared me," he said as Mrs. McGillicuddy walked in the room.

"Make that two people you scared, Grandma." Remington walked away from the tree and hugged her.

"So who's kidding who in here?"

"Uh, nothing, dear," said Mr. McGillicuddy.

"Oh, you know, Grandpa. He always thinks I'm kidding him about something." Remington turned his head toward Mr. McGillicuddy as he continued to hug his grandmother around the waist. He gave him a big wink, and Mr. McGillicuddy smiled.

"Well, the reason I came up here was to tell you something before you went to bed. And by the way, why aren't you in bed? Have you two been talking all this time?"

"Just boys' talk," Mr. McGillicuddy quickly answered and smiled.

"I'm sorry I spoiled our trip to the bullfight."

"It's okay," Remington said before she could go on talking. "Mom and Dad and I had seen the other one, so it was okay. Although, I do kind of wish we could have seen one of the other *matadors.*"

"It was so frightening watching that bull attack the *torero.* Is that the right word, *torero,* or that other word you said?"

"They both mean the same."

"Well, anyway, after that *torero* jumped in front of that poor bull and tried to put that tiny sword or whatever you call that weapon—"

Before she could continue, Remington interrupted. "It is called an *estoque.* I learned that in school.

"Anyway, whatever you call it, the bullfighter misses the poor bull twice, and then on the third try, I guess he finally got the sword to stick in his shoulder blades."

Remington interrupted once more. "I didn't think you saw any of that. You had your hands over your eyes."

"Oh, I saw it. I peeked and saw enough. I heard the crowd booing when he missed the first two times. The poor bull standing there, blood dripping from its mouth.

195

It was moving side to side and about to fall over and that *torero* prancing around in front of him, swooshing that cape back and forth and trying to make him charge again."

"I think we get the idea, dear," Mr. McGillicuddy said. "You didn't enjoy it."

"No, I didn't, but I am sorry, Remington. I know you wanted to see more."

From the doorway came the voice of Remington's father. "I heard all of that."

"Richard, have you been standing out there in the hall eavesdropping?"

"No, not really. I just listened with interest. You know, what we saw today is a big controversy in Spain. Many people think it is a cultural tradition that should continue forever. Others think it is awful and inhumane for the bull."

"Pretty inhumane for that bullfighter," Mr. McGillicuddy said. "He's the one in the hospital with holes in his legs and his belly from the horns of that bull."

"You are right," said Remington's dad. "It is a dangerous sport, although it is not often a *matador* gets gored and injured like you saw today.

"But," Remington's dad continued, "however you want to look at it, bullfighting is both a problem and a bright spot for Spain. But we won't go again. It's okay we left after one bull, and at least you saw what it was like to see all the pageantry and the colors and to even see the king and the royal princess. And, Remington, there were probably more children your age and slightly older there today than normal."

"Why?"

"Because the newly elected president of Spain is going to prohibit persons under fourteen years of age from going to the bullfights when he takes over in a couple of months."

"Well, good for him," said Mrs. McGillicuddy. She smiled, walked to the bed, and bent down and kissed Remington. "Good night, my little redhead." She turned to her husband. "Let's go John. Everyone needs to get some sleep."

"Good night, Grandma. Good night, Grandpa. I love you."

"We love you, too," said Mr. McGillicuddy as the two of them walked out of the room.

"Alright, into bed, young man. It's time to get some sleep," said Remington's dad.

"I know," he said, and slowly crawled up into the bed. "Tomorrow is another big day because we are going to Children's Christmas World at *Plaza del Colón*. I'll get to see all my classmates who were at the party. They tell me it is really a neat place to see and lots of fun."

"I'm sure it is, plus you will get to see all of those acrobats who entertained us. They are part of the show."

"Yippee!"

"But, don't get too excited because I've got something to say to you before you go to sleep."

"What? Why do you have that frown on your face?"

"Because, I'm very disappointed in you."

"And then he scolded Remington, and I'm glad he did."

"Me, too, Bobby," shouted Blinker from the opposite end of the strand.

"Let him talk, Blinker."

"It's okay, Aunt Shining. I know Blinker knows what I am going to say because we talked about it inside Remington's pocket. His dad was angry because of what happened outside the bullfighting stadium." Bobby paused to think how he was going to explain.

"Well, tell us!" bellowed Uncle Flicker, "and make it short. I'm sleepy."

"Calm down, dear," said Aunt Shining.

"We were walking into the stadium, and suddenly I heard Remington say, 'Why don't you get a job?' Then I heard a clanking sound and something bounced across the bricks they were walking on. I know they were bricks because I had heard Mrs. McGillicuddy talking about how beautiful they were and how different from any she had ever seen.

"I heard Remington's mom right after the clanking sound. She yelled to Remington to hurry up and catch up with the four of them. Then Blinker and I started bouncing off each other inside the pocket because Remington started running."

"I still don't understand. What did he do?" asked Bobby's mom.

"That's what Remington's dad was talking to him about. Remington kicked a small can in front of a beggar who was sitting in the middle of the Plaza in front of the bullfighting ring."

"So, what was wrong with that?"

"Oh, Flicker. Be quiet, and listen," said Aunt Shining.

Bobby shouted a little louder, so all the bulbs could definitely hear him. "The homeless person had reached out and touched Remington with a dirty hand. He said something in Spanish that meant he wanted money. Remington jerked his hand loose and kicked the can. It turned over and the few coins inside rolled onto the bricks. That's when Remington yelled at the man to get a job and go to work."

"So, did he get a job?"

Some of the bulbs started laughing, but shut up quickly when Uncle Glimmer scolded Energizer. "There is nothing funny about that."

"Well, the final thing that Remington's dad said, made sense to me," said Bobby. "He told Remington that he had to start understanding that some people can't work. They are handicapped. Some can't find jobs. Others have illnesses. He did say that there are homeless people who are lazy and won't work, but there are always some who simply can't live any other way. His dad told Remington he must try to be more understanding."

"And what did Remington say?" asked Aunt Glaring.

"That those people were still dirty and needed a bath. It was then that Remington's dad stood up from the bed and told Remington they would talk some more about it, but he had better be more understanding."

All of the bulbs remained quiet and said nothing. When Bobby didn't continue, Uncle Flicker said, "Now, can we get some sleep?"

24

Countdown to New Year's Eve

Remington finished the last bite of a pancake his mom had fixed him. "These pancakes are great, Lisa," said Mrs. McGillicuddy. "I don't know why they are so different, but they have a better taste than the ones back home."

"I love them too, Grandma."

"Oh, I think that's pretty evident. What was that one? Your fourth?"

Remington tucked his head for a moment and then looked up and smiled. "Nope, my fifth," he said, and he got up from the table and started to leave the room.

"Get your warmest jacket and hurry back down here," said his mom. "We are leaving for Children's World in fifteen minutes. And"—she said to Mrs. McGillicuddy—"you definitely need to wear that long coat of yours with the furry collar."

"Oh, I know, dear," she answered. "I walked out on our balcony for about ten seconds before breakfast, and it is cold. I can't believe it is two degrees below zero."

Remington was only a few feet outside the kitchen door in the hallway, and he quickly ducked back into the room. "It's not below zero."

"Well, that's what that sign you pointed out to me read. It's the one in front of that bank at the bottom of the hill."

"I know the sign, Grandma."

"Well, I saw it just a few minutes ago, and it read only two degrees."

"That is Celsius, Grandma," Remington explained proudly. "It's not close to zero Fahrenheit."

Mrs. McGillicuddy looked up with a surprise. "Oh, that's right; it's different here. I keep forgetting."

"Actually, it's about thirty-five degrees Fahrenheit, but still plenty cold, and probably going to get colder," said Lisa.

"See, Grandma, I told you," and he ran out of the room.

His mom yelled after him. "Where are you going?"

"Back to get Bobby."

"Whoa, little boy. No Bobby, today."

"But, Mom. Why?"

"You are in for a surprise, young man. Get your coat and get back down here. While we are at Children's World and at *Parque del Retiro* today, something is going to happen here at the apartment, and you will be surprised."

"A surprise?"

"Just get your coat. Your dad will tell you."

Remington, followed by his dad, came up the stairs to the second floor. He yelled back over his shoulder, "I love you, too, Mom. Love you, Grandpa and Grandma."

"So were the acrobats and entertainers even better than you thought they would be at Children's World?"

"Oh yeah." He turned and stopped in the hallway outside his bedroom door. "They were amazing. I thought Grandma was going to faint for a moment when those three angels came flying over the top of that giant wall behind the plaza. It really did look like they were flying."

"I know," said his dad. "You couldn't even see those cable wires that they were attached to."

"Remember when Grandpa and I asked you what that huge crane was for, the one sitting behind the park?"

"Why did you say it was there to help build a tall building?"

"I just wanted to surprise the two of you."

"Yeah, but the best part was when the three clowns flew over the audience and nearly touched our heads before they landed on the stage."

"Well, it's a marvelous show, and children in Madrid are very lucky to get that kind of entertainment every Christmas. Now, it's time for bed. Get in there. And Mom said to tell you to put on a clean pair of pajamas."

Remington walked into the dark bedroom, turned on the light, and headed for the chest of drawers near the closet. He had just started to open the top drawer when he suddenly turned and screamed, "Oh no! Where are they?"

Before he could continue, his dad walked quickly to him, bent down on one knee, and put his left arm around Remington's shoulder. "Don't panic."

"Daddy, where are my Christmas tree lights? Where are the bulbs?"

"It's the reason I walked up here with you. I have a surprise, so don't get worried."

"But where are they?"

"Come on," put your pajamas on, and we will go back downstairs. Don't panic. You will see."

Inside the first floor closet it was pitch black. It was much darker than the closet where the bulbs had been boxed up all those years at the McGillicuddys'.

"This is the darkest place ever. It is so scary. I know we haven't been here very long, but it seems like forever."

"I know, Mom, but it is going to be okay. We may have to stay here until tomorrow, but what we are connected to has to be the box that Remington's dad talked about. It's the reason we will get to be with Remington for New Year's Eve."

"Well, I wish it would hurry and get here."

"Have patience, Aunt Glaring. It will be worth it, I'm sure."

The door opened, and the light was turned on. "Please let me peek, Daddy."

"Remington McGillicuddy. You get back over there and sit down next to your grandparents right now."

"Okay, but can't you hurry?"

"As soon as you get on the other side of the room," Remington's Dad said. He stood in front of the open door and prevented Remington from peeking inside.

Remington walked slowly to the opposite side.

"Come on, sit on my lap," said his grandmother. "You are really going to be surprised." Remington sat down. "Whoa, you are too heavy. Sit between Grandpa and me."

He sat down and then started to laugh. "Wow! You look funny, Daddy. Why are my Christmas tree lights wrapped around your body and head?"

Everyone in the room started to laugh. Remington's mom was laughing the hardest. "Richard, you look absolutely silly or maybe it's stupid. One thing is for sure; it's not normal."

"What are you doing with my bulbs?"

When his dad started to answer, Mr. McGillicuddy jumped up off the couch and said, "I'm going to get the camera. You look absolutely nutty."

"Okay, Remington, come here." His dad motioned with his hands to walk over to him. "These will look better on you."

Remington walked to his father. "What do you mean?"

"Just listen! This is my surprise for you. That goofy granddad of yours has all of us believing that your bulbs can do magical things. So I thought if they are that special, let's take them to one of the greatest New Year's Eve celebrations in the world."

"What? You mean they are all coming with me tomorrow night, not just Bobby?"

"That's right."

Then Remington's dad began to remove the bulbs from around his waist and from around his shoulders and head, and he bent down and put them on Remington. He clipped the small silver metal box to Remington's belt. "This is where the power comes," he told Remington.

"Will you look at that," said Mr. McGillicuddy as he walked into the room holding his camera. "Do you ever look fancy and a hundred times better than your father."

"Remington, with all the wild costumes for New Years Eve, you will be our walking Christmas tree and fit right in with everyone."

"Are you speechless?" asked Mrs. McGillicuddy.

A smile broke out on Remington's face. "I guess a little bit. This is amazing. Oh, Daddy, what a surprise. Thank you."

"You're welcome. You are going to be the brightest-looking person in Madrid."

"Where's Bobby?" Remington tiptoed across the room and looked in the mirror on the wall near the front door. "Oh, there. I see you," he said as he saw his reflection in the mirror. He reached up and touched the blue bulb, which was sitting right on top of his head. "That's a perfect spot for you."

Then he turned around and looked at everyone. "If I'm going to be the brightest-looking kid in Madrid, then he must be"—he reached up and touched the blue bulb—"Bobby Bright."

"*Can you believe it?*"

"*I know, Mom. It was weird hearing my name come from his voice, and even stranger when his folks and grandparents said, 'That's a perfect name for your special bulb.'*"

"*You are our hero again. If it weren't for you, we would never have gotten this chance.*"

"*Thanks, Sparkle, but I just want all of us to enjoy tomorrow night. Now, let's get to sleep.*"

Across the room, tucked in his bed, with only a few strands of red hair showing from beneath the covers,

Remington McGillicuddy snored slightly and mumbled something in his sleep.

"Maybe he's dreaming about tomorrow night," whispered Bobby. "It sure should be something special for all of us."

25
New Year's Eve Day

It was one o'clock in the afternoon, the time most Spaniards start thinking about lunch. As the McGillicuddys had also learned, it was not uncommon for people to wait as late as three or three thirty for their midday meal.

"You are not eating until you get that room cleaned up, Remington."

"I know, Mom. Granddaddy and I are headed upstairs right now. He's going to help me."

"I am? Are you sure I'm going to help?"

"Oh, you're just teasing me. I know you will." The two of them trudged up the stairs to the second floor.

"I'm so excited about tonight. We are going to have a wonderful *Nochevieja* celebration."

"I've heard you say that word before," Mr. McGillicuddy said as the two of them walked into Remington's bedroom. It was strange looking at the tree and not seeing the bulbs, Remington thought.

"Does that mean New Year's Eve?"

"Yeah, Grandpa. *Nochevieja.*"

"Well, I hope we have a great Nocha Veecha," said Mr. McGillicuddy.

Remington started laughing immediately.

"What's so funny?"

Remington laughed harder. "You're so funny. No-chay vee-ay-ha. That's how you pronounce New Year's Eve in Spanish."

"That's what I said, Nocha Veecha."

Remington was laughing so hard he began to cough and choke. "Are you all right?" Mr. McGillicuddy raced across the room and grabbed him. He patted him on his back with the palm of his hand. "Did you swallow something? What's wrong?"

"Nothing," said Remington as he tried to quit laughing. "It's just you. You are so funny."

"Why, because I said Nocha Veecha?"

Remington dropped and twisted across the floor, like a rolling pin out of control. He was still laughing and gyrating on the floor when Mrs. McGillicuddy walked into the room. "Are you all right, Remington?"

Remington rolled onto his side and looked up at her. Tears rolled down his cheeks. He wiped them away and said, "I'm okay, Grandma."

"Why has he been crying?"

Before Mr. McGillicuddy could answer, Remington said, "I'm okay. It's just Grandpa. He is so funny."

"Now what have you done, John?"

"Nothing, dear."

"Oh, you did something, all right. Otherwise, Remington wouldn't be laughing like this."

"It's just the way he says *Nochevieja*. It sounds funny."

"You mean New Year's Eve in Spanish?"

"See, even Grandma knows how to say it."

"Well, John, you go down and help Lisa set the table. Remington, get this room cleaned up quickly. You can tell me about tonight while you are working, but hurry up; I'm hungry."

Remington and his grandmother visited for ten minutes while he slowly picked up his clothes and made his bed and gathered up some old papers lying in the closet.

"That sounds so different. Everyone eats grapes at midnight?"

"Yep. Daddy says it will be fun. You know, my friend Aaron told me it was great last year. He said he couldn't believe how much fun it was. He's a year older than me, and he said when he was really young he remembered being with his parents in Times Square in New York. He said there were so many people that he had to sit on his dad's shoulders so he could see. Last year, he said his parents told him there were thousands and thousands more people at *Puerta del* Sol than in Times Square."

"Well, no matter how many people there are, I'm sure it will be exciting. Now, are you finished?"

"I think so," he said and looked around the room. He picked up a dirty shirt and some socks off the floor and headed for the door. "Let's go eat."

Remington wiped his mouth. "Thank you," said his mom. "The juice was running down your chin."

"I know. But, it's hard not to get juice on you when you eat *pollo del horno*. You know what we say, Mom and Daddy; it's the juice that makes the chicken so good."

"You're right. It is excellent. What you just said means roast chicken, right?"

"Yep, Grandma. Like Mom says, 'Nobody makes rotisserie chicken like the Spanish.'"

"It was excellent, Lisa," Mr. McGillicuddy said as he stood up to leave the table.

"Sit down, Grandpa. Daddy wants to explain how we eat the grapes tonight."

"Grapes? Have you got some more of those grapes, Lisa? They're delicious," Mr. McGillicuddy said.

"No more until tonight," she answered. "Save your good luck for midnight."

"The Spanish really believe it brings good luck?"

"Yes, they do."

"Tell them the story, Dad."

"Well, there is more than one story. And sometimes you hear different versions. But basically here's what happened. Early in the last century—I think it was 1909— the grape crop in Spain was the largest in history. There were so many grapes that the farms and giant estates couldn't sell all of them.

"A decision was made to destroy the remaining grapes. However, some government officials decided rather than waste the grapes, it would be better to give them away or find a creative way to sell them as the year came to a close.

"So throughout many parts of Spain, where there were large amounts of excess grapes, people had a chance to get large bunches for free or for very little cost. Someone came up with the idea that they could make the grapes a part of the New Year's Eve celebration. It was decided each person would take a dozen grapes, and as the clock tolled toward midnight, a grape would be swallowed, one at a time, during the final twelve seconds of the old year. This eating of the grapes was supposed to bring good luck for the coming year and represented the twelve months of the calendar.

"The idea was so popular that more people did it the next year, and even though grapes weren't ever given away in large quantities again, the eating of the grapes became a traditional part of welcoming in the New Year. As time has gone on, some people even make a wish as they swallow each of the grapes. There are some who believe that if you don't eat all of the dozen grapes in the final twelve seconds, your wishes or good luck won't come true.

"Most importantly, it has become a wonderful tradition, and I really believe the grapes in Spain are much
more of a New Year's tradition than black-eyed peas are
in our country.

"Now, that's enough about the grapes. Remington, you
need to go take a nap right now. This is going to be a long
night, and it will be two or three in the morning before
we get back to the apartment."

26

A Celebration to Remember

It was indeed a night to remember. By the time Remington and his family had walked from the apartment on *Fomento* to *Gran Via,* there had already been at least twenty people pointing and smiling at the little boy who had bulbs wrapped around his body and around the top of the cap on his head. Once the family had finished walking the five blocks up the hill on *Gran Via* to *Calle de Preciados,* over three hundred people had already been cheering and pointing at Remington.

When they entered the long, wide pedestrian avenue, the cheers of *"Brilliante," "Fantástico," "Increíble," "Magnífico,"* and *"Que interesante"* greeted the McGillicuddys. And those chants of "brilliant," "fantastic," "incredible," "magnificent," and "how interesting" followed them as they worked their way through thousands of party goers headed to the main plaza of *Puerta del Sol* for the midnight celebration.

It was a journey all five of them would talk about for years to come.

The noise was nearly as loud as the terrible tornado that had struck the McGillicuddys' house last year. But this time Bobby and the bulbs could see what was happening, and while it was a little scary with all of the people Remington kept bumping into, it was amazing what they saw and heard.

"*Unbelievable,*" bellowed Uncle Flicker, although Bobby barely heard him with the din of noise as people cheered and whistled, and the sounds of those long horns blared throughout the plaza.

"*It's so noisy, Aunt Glaring. Did you hear who that was?*"

"*Oh, it was Flicker. He's at the other end, right next to that box on Remington's hip. He's staring right into a lot of bodies bumping up against him.*"

"*Bobby, this is so exciting,*" shouted his mom. "*And your dad has the biggest smile I've ever seen on his face. Twist and take a look.*"

Bobby did just that. "*Hey, Dad! Can you believe this noise and all those funny-looking wigs on these people?*" Everywhere they looked there were men, women, and lots of children wearing big afro-like purple, green, blue, orange, and red wigs. Lots of beads hung from people's necks, and many of the children were blowing big, long-stemmed horns that made lots of noise.

Suddenly, Bobby felt a hand come over the top of the cap. It was Remington. And through all the noise, Bobby heard him say, "Be careful up there, Bobby. We are in the main plaza and almost to where we are going."

"*Sigame, señor. Tienen plazos al mitad de esta sección.*" Then he smiled and shook the hand of Remington's dad. "*Hay plazos reservados para el pez gordo.*"

Remington's dad started laughing and patted the usher on the shoulder. Then he turned to his family and said, "Follow me. He's showing us to our seats. They are all reserved."

Mr. McGillicuddy was first in line behind his son and asked him, "Why are you laughing?"

"Oh, the usher used a phrase in Spanish that means big wig or very important person."

"What's funny about that?"

"Well, if you translate it word for word in Spanish," Richard said, "it means big fish."

Mr. McGillicuddy smiled and said, "Well, from the looks of things, you must be more important at that embassy than even we thought you were. It looks like we are going to be right in the middle of the reviewing stand."

"This was part of my promise last year when I accepted the job. We would get airline tickets early so we could give them to you as a surprise, and we would get some special favors when you visited."

"Well," Mr. McGillicuddy said, "I would call this a special favor."

The usher stopped at the tenth step on the stairway. They were halfway to the top of the hundred-yard-long section of bleachers.

"*Se diviertan el espectáculo, señor. Sientense.*" He pointed to the first five seats off of the aisle.

"*Gracias, y próspero año nuevo,*" said Remington's dad.

"*A usted, señor, y su familia igualmente.*"

As the McGillicuddys took their seats, the noise around them got louder. There were dancers preparing to perform in the open area in front of the bleachers. Mrs. McGillicuddy raised her voice. "What did that man say, Richard?"

"He just said to enjoy the show."

"That's not all, Grandma. He also said to 'take these seats,' and to have a happy New Year."

"Well, thank you, Mr. Translator." Mrs. McGillicuddy smiled and bent down and gave Remington a kiss on the forehead. Then she did the strangest thing.

"*What was that all about?*" Aunt Glaring asked. She began to laugh, and so did Bobby. He twisted so he could see her, his mom, dad, brother, two sisters, and Flash.

They were the eight bulbs that lay in a circle atop Remington's cap.

He shouted, "*Do you want to hear something funny?*"

Dimmer answered first. "*Sure, Bobby.*"

"*After Mrs. McGillicuddy kissed Remington on the forehead, she reached up and touched me. You probably saw that. Then she bent down, and if you didn't see what happened next,*" he continued, "*she put a kiss right on the top of my head. And then, she told me 'Happy New Year.'*"

"*You know,*" his mom said, "*if you are worth a kiss, you must be special.*"

"*Well, we already knew that,*" said Aunt Glaring.

"*Oh, please, you are embarrassing me.*"

"*We will never be able to thank you enough. I wish we could celebrate New Year's Eve every year if it's like this.*"

"*I think we better consider ourselves lucky and enjoy the moment. This won't happen again,*" said Bobby's dad.

And he was right. Never would there ever be a New Year's Eve like this one for the Bright family or for the McGillicuddys.

"Richard, Lisa, we can't thank you enough. It was unbelievable, and you were right about the grapes. What a tradition. I didn't know if I could swallow all twelve of them in such a short time."

"Did you make a wish each time, Grandma?"

"I tried to, Remington."

"So did I, Remington," Mr. McGillicuddy joined in. "But I didn't do as good as the rest of you."

"It's okay. As long as you ate all twelve of them, it will be okay."

"So do you think all those wishes I made will come true?"

"What were they, Grandpa?"

"Well, I can't tell you that or they won't have a chance to come true."

"Richard, Lisa, that was such a wonderful show. All those people and those wonderful dancers and entertainers in front of the bleachers were just marvelous. And the fireworks show after midnight was the greatest I have ever seen anywhere," added Mrs. McGillicuddy.

"It's time for you to go to bed, Remington," his mom interrupted. "It's 1:30, and your grandparents need to visit about something with Daddy and me."

"I'm not tired. Why can't I listen?"

"Because this is adult business and something that one day might be a surprise for you."

"But what about my hot chocolate? You were going to get me some more."

"Take those bulbs off and lay them someplace in your room. Don't put them on the tree, because you may wear them to the big parade after we get back from our trip. Now, you get upstairs right now. I will bring you the hot chocolate when I tuck you in."

27

Story of a New Year's Discovery

After putting Remington to bed, Richard returned to the living room and placed four cups on the living room coffee table. He sat down on the maroon sofa to enjoy the hot chocolate. "I've got an interesting story to tell you."

"Is anything wrong, dear?" Mrs. McGillicuddy asked.

"It depends on how much you meant about feeling sorry for someone, Mom. Remember on the way home? You know the long pedestrian boulevard, *Calle de Preciados?*" His parents nodded their heads. "Well, we had just left the boulevard and turned onto *Gran Via,* but I got caught at the stoplight and fell behind."

Lisa said, "I remember turning around and not seeing you and thought you had fallen behind. I got a bit scared because I couldn't see you, but then, a block later, you caught up with us. I saw you running and pushing your way through the crowd."

"I never even knew," said Mrs. McGillicuddy. "Remington and I were having too much fun watching the people point at the lights wrapped around him. So why did you stop or fall behind us?"

"I had just passed that huge movie theater with the eight glass doors and the marble steps. It was then I caught a glimpse of something out of the corner of my eye. That's when I dropped back and the four of you kept going.

"This is really kind of weird. Near one of those huge boxes that the homeless people stay in, I saw what looked like part of a sweater lying just outside one of the flaps that covered up the box. It was like an entrance."

"A sweater made you stop?" asked Mr. McGillicuddy.

"Yeah, Dad, because the sweater looked just like one mom had when she got here two weeks ago."

He started to explain, but Mrs. McGillicuddy quickly said, "Oh my heavens! Are you getting ready to say what I think you are, Richard?"

"Yes, I am, Mom. I'm sure you know. It was the homeless woman who claimed she saw a bulb flying over Remington."

"What does—"

Before Mrs. McGillicuddy could ask the question, he continued, "Let me tell the rest of the story, and then we can talk about what is going to happen.

"I walked six steps up to the landing, and I bent down to make sure it was what I thought it was. It was pretty dark even though the glow from the bulbs in the theater lobby cast some light near the edge of the box. Just as I reached down to touch the sweater, a hand reached out and flipped up an old blanket hanging over the side of the box. There she was. It was no doubt. The same one you brought the sweaters and the two dresses to at the police station.

"She had a frightened look on her face, and she screamed, '*¡No me daño!* I held up my hand and said in Spanish, 'I won't hurt you.' Then—"

But Mrs. McGillicuddy broke in before he could say another word. "Richard, if you are going to tell us to be quiet, then you must tell us what the Spanish words mean."

"She said, 'Don't hurt me.' I told her I wouldn't." Richard paused for a moment and took a long swallow of hot chocolate.

"Well, tell us what happened."

"It didn't take very long. I asked her if she was okay, and she said yes in a very sad voice. I started to say, 'Happy New Year' to her, but that sounded stupid. How could anyone be happy in that box, all alone and cold? And then she surprised me by saying, '*Próspero año nuevo.*'" He looked directly at his mother. "That means Happy New Year."

She looked right back into his eyes and said, "Thank you."

"I must have looked surprised because she then said the strangest thing."

"What?" Mrs. McGillicuddy gulped.

224

"She said, '*Tenga cuidado, señor.*' That means 'Be careful, sir.' She had the saddest look on her face. I started to say something else, but she began to crawl back into the box."

"Did you stop her?" asked Mr. McGillicuddy.

Mrs. McGillicuddy frowned at her husband. "John, we agreed to be quiet until he is finished."

Richard continued with the story. "Yes, I convinced her to talk a little longer. It's why I was late in catching up with you. I said to her, 'What do you mean?' and she told me that just two years ago she was a teacher in a small town in far northern Spain, near the French border. A huge ice storm hit in the mountains, and there was an ice-packed river that flooded and destroyed part of the town. She lost her house, and her husband was killed. She had only a few Euros in the bank. There was no life insurance, and she ended up losing all of her possessions. She had enough for a train ride to Madrid, but when she got here there were no jobs for her. She ran out of money and for the last year has lived on the street, begging for food and money, and was able to work only a few times. Most of the work was cleaning out toilets at the movie theater."

He stopped talking and looked at his wife and parents. They said nothing but all had sad looks, and then he saw his mother start to cry. "You mean that poor woman was a teacher?"

"Yes."

225

"Then, Richard, you listen to me. We have to do something for her."

"I hoped you would say that, Mom, because I told her I would be back to see her in five days."

"Five days," Mrs. McGillicuddy shouted. "We can't leave her there for five days."

"Mother, we are taking our trip tomorrow. When we return, she will be there."

"How do you know?"

"Because"—and then he smiled—"I told her we had a trip planned for my son and his grandparents and I could see her again when we got back. I told her I wanted to help her, and she said, 'Go with your family. That is the most important thing. This old woman will still be here,' and then just like that"—Richard snapped the middle finger of his right hand against his thumb—"she crawled into the box and pulled the old blanket across the front."

28
A Quick Trip and a Big Surprise

On the morning of January second, the McGillicuddy's left for a whirlwind three-day visit of Spain that took them to a sailing capital, famous for a great Spanish food, to a tiny seaside village, and a historic old town with a famous old castle perched above it on a mountainside.

"I haven't been on a train in many, many years," said Mrs. McGillicuddy. This will be fun," she added as the family walked into the Atocha train station.

"This will be my fifth train trip since we moved to Spain," Remington said excitedly. "Everyone rides the train in Spain."

Suddenly Remington pulled away from his grandparents and ran to his mom. He whispered something to her and started to point.

"What's wrong, Lisa?" Mrs. McGillicuddy shouted from a few feet away.

But before she could answer, Remington's dad hollered from the turnstile where the passengers enter the area where the track platforms are, "Hurry up. The ticket taker needs to tear your tickets. Let's go!"

Three days later, as the train pulled into the Atocha station in Madrid, the five weary travelers were still talking about a trip they would remember forever. The world-famous Spanish dish, Paella, which they ate in big servings in Valencia. Walking the streets of *Peñíscola* and looking down at the sandy beaches below. And Mrs. McGillicuddy's favorite town of *Morella*, where she purchased a suitcase full of new sweaters for all of her friends back home in America.

It was 10:15 p.m. as the five exhausted travelers walked through the terminal. Remington suddenly grabbed his mom's hand and pulled her back behind the others. He pointed to a dirty corner of the main station that was cluttered with old papers and pieces of thrown away food.

"There she is. I saw her again, Mom, just like I did three days ago. She was in a different place, just around that corner."

"Who are you talking about?"

"The old homeless lady, and she had on one of grandma's old dresses she gave her, but it was dirty. She waved at me."

"Did you wave back?"

"No. She looks bad."

"Remington. Don't be ugly. She doesn't have a real home."

"What's going on? Hurry up," Remington's dad called back to them. The taxi is waiting."

"Let's go," said his mom. You need to get some sleep so you will be ready for the Three Kings Parade tomorrow."

29

Cabalgata De Los Reyes Magos

Throughout the world in countries that celebrate the twelve days of Christmas, January fifth is a day children wait for with high expectation.

"Well, it must really be special because you've talked about it a lot," said Mrs. McGillicuddy.

"I know. I'm really excited. My buddies at school told me the Three Kings throw lots of candy to all the children along the parade route, and the parade lasts for at least three hours."

"You mean we are going to be watching a parade for three hours?" Mr. McGillicuddy had just walked into the room and immediately headed to the kitchen counter where the plate with the *roscón de reyes* was sitting.

"Yes, I am so excited. There are all kinds of floats, people walking on high stilts, clowns, dancers, even some trained animals, camels, horses, and—"

Remington paused to catch his breath, but before he could continue, Mr. McGillicuddy said, "Whoa! Stop! If you're going to tell me everything, it won't be a surprise."

Remington's father walked into the kitchen. "Is there any of that Christmas cake left?"

"Not very much, dear," Mrs. McGillicuddy answered. "Do we have another one of those cakes? John has nearly eaten all of this one. Remington, how do you pronounce it again?"

"It's pronounced, '*Rows-cone de ray-es.*'"

Mrs. McGillicuddy smiled. "I think I'll just call it the round cake with all the fruit and goodies." Remington giggled, his dad smiled, and Mr. McGillicuddy laughed.

Remington's mom walked into the kitchen and said, "The bigger question is not whether Grandma can say *roscón de reyes* correctly, it is whether your granddaddy has eaten all of it."

Mr. McGillicuddy's face reddened, and he brushed some cake crumbs from his chin. He started to speak, but Mrs. McGillicuddy said, "There are still more crumbs on your face. Wipe those off too."

"Where?"

"How about right on the end of your nose?"

"Oh," he said and reached up with his left hand. He brushed more pieces of cake off the tip of his nose and then said, "Lisa, is there another cake? This one's gone."

"You're lucky," Remington's mom said and pulled another *roscon* from the pantry drawer near the stove.

"Oh, would you look at that," said Mr. McGillicuddy. "That is the most beautiful one yet."

"Oh, Lisa! John is right. Look at all of the fruit on top, and Remington, this cake has two beans sticking out of the side. This one must really be lucky."

"I've got a feeling," said Remington's dad, "we will all feel lucky and fortunate after we see the *Cabalgata de los Reyes Magos* tonight."

It was nearly six o'clock in the afternoon. The parade was minutes from starting. "We have a difficult decision," said Remington's dad. The McGillicuddys were sitting in their reserved seats, right in the center of a long row of bleachers. Many of the spectators were already looking at Remington, who was wearing all of the Christmas tree lights like he had done on New Years Eve.

"How can anything be difficult with this view?" Mr. McGillicuddy said. "You told us we are right in front of the spot where all the entertainers stop and perform."

"I know, but listen," he said, and he leaned around Mr. McGillicuddy so Remington, Lisa, and Mrs. McGillicuddy could hear. "We also have a chance, thanks to my friends at the embassy, to go to the area at the end of the parade. That's where the Three Kings give their speeches to the crowd. There are also some guest entertainers from China and Italy. They are supposed to be amazing acts. It's like the closing ceremonies of the parade."

"Oh, Daddy, let's go there for that part. That way we can see the Three Kings when they throw out more candy."

Before Remington's dad could answer, one of his friends from the embassy came down the aisle from the opposite side. "Ricardo," he said and then began speaking in rapid Spanish to Remington's father.

"What was that all about?"

"Well, honey, that was Juan Garcia from the embassy. He overheard us talking. He says that just before the Three Kings arrive at this location, four officials at the embassy are going to be taken by van to the *Plaza Cibeles* where the parade ends. They will be on the stage with the kings for their final speeches. So we are going to get to ride with them and sit right in front of the stage. We will have first row seats."

"Isn't it great to be a *pez gordo?*" Remington's mom said and hugged her husband. Then they laughed and reminded Remington and his grandparents again that "very important person" in English translated to "fat fish" in Spanish.

"They may be the Three Kings of Orient," said Mr. McGillicuddy, "but we are the Five Fat Fish.'" Just as they started to laugh, the loud blare of trumpets was heard, and the first floats and parade marchers could be seen two blocks away.

Two hours into the most amazing parade he had ever seen, Remington squealed and hugged his dad for about the fifteenth time. "This parade is even better than those we watch on television on Thanksgiving Day."

"Look out," said Mr. McGillicuddy, who was sitting next to Remington. "You are stepping on me."

"Oh, John, quit acting like you are a child. He's just excited."

"Well, I want to see everything. This is the greatest parade I've ever seen too. Look, Remington, what's coming down the road."

"This is not a road, Grandpa. It's *Paseo de Castellana,* the widest street in all of Madrid."

Remington let out a yelp when he saw what his grandfather was pointing to. "Oh my gosh! Look at that dragon." He reached across and pulled on his grandmother's arm. She was busy watching the cyclists who were riding ten-foot-high bicycles with giant front wheels and very small rear wheels.

"Look, Remington, don't you think they are going to fall off?"

"Yes, but look what is coming."

When she turned her head, she too gasped. "Oh my gracious!"

"See."

234

The dragon, with meticulously painted patterns of red, orange, green, and black, was at least 150 feet long and was carried by brightly clad walkers, who had on tight-fitting gold pants and fluffy, multicolored shirts and blouses. As they danced underneath the creature, its tail moved from side to side.

"Unbelievable," said Mr. McGillicuddy. "How in the world did they ever make anything so big?"

"Thanks for bringing us to Spain, Daddy!" Remington shrieked.

"Enjoy this because we won't ever see a parade this great again. Juan told me a few minutes ago that there is also a huge fish just like this dragon. So we will get to see another one of these before the night is over. He says it takes about fifty people to carry each of them.

"They are made with tightly wrapped wires that are covered with a thick papier-mâché-type fabric. Then it takes weeks to paint them."

"Look, Bobby," squealed Remington, and he reached up with his hands and touched the bulbs on top of his cap. "I hope all of you can see this."

The people on the reviewing stand were on their feet, standing and applauding wildly as the head of the twisting fifty-foot-high colorful dragon actually dipped all the way to the ground when the walkers dropped to their knees. There was another huge round of applause from the other side of the five lane wide avenue. There were hundreds of spectators standing five and six rows deep opposite the bleachers. They were just a small part of the tens of thousands of Spaniards who were enjoying the *Cabalgata*. The parade had started at the axis of *Castellana* more than two miles from the reviewing stand. It would eventually conclude at the *Plaza Cibeles*.

There were nearly three hundred cyclists, dancers, acrobats, men, and women on fifteen-foot-high stilts, horseback riders, and over fifty magnificent floats. And of course, at the end of the parade, the Three Kings riding on camels would deliver their brief but famous speeches to the crowd.

Remington continued to watch the dragon as the walkers carried it on down the five lane wide avenue. He didn't feel the touch of his mom's fingers on his shoulder the first time when she said, "Remington, look at me. Don't look at the parade for a moment." When he didn't turn his head, she tapped him on his shoulder again. "Remington. Look at me!"

"But there is too much to see."

"Just look at me. Remember when Daddy and I told you not to get the big head when you made all those straight A's on your report card last year?"

"Yeah, Mom," he said and turned to look at her. "But what's that got to do with the parade?"

"I just wanted to tell you"—she and Mrs. McGillicuddy started laughing—"I just wanted to tell you that sometimes it's okay to have the big head."

"Mom, what are you talking about?"

"See," she said. "Turn around and look."

When Remington looked back, he saw in front of the bleachers the first of a long line of marchers with ten- to fifteen-foot-high poles. They were hoisted in the air, and at the top of each pole was another papier-mâché figure. Only this time, it wasn't a fish or a dragon; it was a smiling face. Large heads with different faces were everywhere, carried by marchers who bobbed the poles up and down to the rhythm of the music from a nearby band.

There were grins, frowns, smiles, large noses, small noses, big eyes, small eyes, and fat cheeks. Each one was different. And each one brought oohs and aahs from the crowd. "They are magnificent and funny too," said Mr. McGillicuddy.

And funny costumes, great dancers, marvelous performers, and three stunningly attired kings made the evening one they would remember forever.

"*Did you see the size of those heads on those tall poles?*"

"*Yes, I did, Dimmer,*" said Bobby. "*Do you remember hearing Remington laugh when he realized what his mom meant?*"

"*What's 'big head' mean again, Bobby?*" Twinkle asked.

"It's a human saying for someone who thinks he is smarter or better than other people when he really isn't."

"Those faces were gigantic. I thought one of them looked like Mr. McGillicuddy."

"Oh, Bingo, only you would think that."

"No, I really did think it. Remember the one with the funny-looking eyebrows? It was the one that kept falling over, and the marchers would put it back up on the pole. Well, that's the one that reminded me of Mr. McGillicuddy because he is always falling over, falling down, or doing something goofy."

"Now, I understand what you mean."

"Hey, Bobby, how about that huge long fish, the one that was just as big as that dragon?"

"I thought it was even prettier than the dragon, Flash."

"I liked it even more because the mouth of the fish kept moving up and down like it was trying to breathe or eat something."

And so it went for an hour and a half as the bulbs lay on Remington's bed, remembering the amazing parade. They were stretched from the top of the pillow to the foot of the bed, placed there by Remington when he had removed them from around his body and his cap.

Remington was downstairs having a special dinner. When the McGillicuddy family had first returned home from the parade, Remington's mom had said, "I want you to take those bulbs off right now, wash your hands and face, and get ready for dinner. Everything was prepared before we left, so I only have to warm it up."

But Remington had first gone to the kitchen and selected a knife from the drawer. He had walked to the table and was about to slice a piece of *roscón de reyes*. "What do you think you are doing with that knife?"

"I'll be careful. I just need to get a piece of cake ready for the Three Kings. All the kids at school have told me you must leave candy or some kind of treat for them when they bring presents tonight."

"You also have to leave a pair of shoes by the door so they can place the presents near them. So you need to go get your new dress shoes and put them by the front door."

Mrs. McGillicuddy came into the kitchen. She and Mr. McGillicuddy had taken their coats upstairs to their bedroom when they first returned from the parade. "Shoes by the door," she declared. "What is that all about?"

"When I wake up in the morning, there will be presents by my shoes. The Three Kings will leave them, and while they are here, they will want something to eat. So I'm leaving them a slice of the *roscón*.

"Don't you remember, Grandma, when we were driving in from the airport the first day? I told you Santa Claus doesn't come every place in Spain like he does in the United States. The sixth of January, the Epiphany, which is the twelfth day of Christmas, is the big day for receiving gifts."

"So, you are saying shoes, sweets, kings, and presents are what it's all about, huh?"

"You got it, Grandma."

30

A Big Surprise for
Mr. and Mrs. McGillicuddy

It didn't feel right. Even though it wasn't Christmas like in the United States, it was the day most children in Spain opened their Christmas gifts. So, being a Christmas tree light bulb on a strand laying on a bedspread and stretched across a bed, instead of on a tree, was a very different thing.

"This is kind of weird," said Aunt Glaring.

"You mean being off the tree instead of on it?" asked Bobby.

"Exactly. Look! I think Remington is waking up. It's time for a very different Christmas day for him."

"I wonder what time it is." Remington sat up in bed, looked at the dresser and saw the clock read, January 6, 7:45 a.m. "Oh, boy! I'm going to find out what the Three Kings left me." He jumped out of bed and raced to the closet, grabbed his robe, and stepped into his house slippers.

He hurried down the stairs. He didn't expect to see anyone because he thought they would still be sleeping after staying up late last night. When he jumped off the bottom step of the stairs, he saw his dress shoes next to the front door. He also saw an empty plate where the *roscón de reyes* had been placed the night before. Three empty glasses sat next to the shoes. He had insisted there be milk for every king. They had to share the *roscón*.

Now, he ran to the door, bent over, and picked up the pair of dress shoes. He peered into each of them. There was nothing inside. When he looked up, he hollered, "Oh, you scared me. I didn't know you were there."

Across the room, half hidden behind a tall, three-paneled room divider, stood his smiling grandparents.

"Surprise!"

He turned his head to the right and saw his parents rise up from behind the sofa.

"Why are you already dressed? And why didn't the Three Kings leave me anything? Do you have to be a Spaniard to get a gift?"

"Calm down," said Remington's dad. "You didn't look very closely at that dish where you left the *roscón*, did you?"

"What do you mean? It's empty."

"Go back and take a look."

He retraced his steps back to the front door. He looked at the plate. "There's still nothing here."

"Pick it up," said his mom.

He bent down and picked up the plate. At first he didn't feel anything, but when his fingers moved around the edge, he touched something. He looked at his grandfather, who was smiling. "What is it?" His fingers were touching something that felt like paper. He turned the plate over and saw a small envelope taped to the bottom.

"Come sit down and open the envelope," ordered his dad.

"Is this my surprise from the Three Kings?"

"In a way it is. They actually left you some big chunks of candy and another *roscón* with three lucky beans on top. We've already put it in the kitchen because we wanted you to see this letter. It is our gift to you, and when you read it, you will realize it is a gift to all of us and especially to the person who wrote the letter."

"Wow, this is an exciting mystery for a nine-year-old," he said.

There were chuckles from everyone.

"Okay, here goes." He tore open the back of the envelope. There was a letter inside, and he removed it. It was folded just once. "Daddy, this is in Spanish."

"Just the title, and you know enough Spanish to understand that. The rest is in English. It's not perfect English, but you will understand. Do you know what it says?"

"Yes. It says '*Mi amigo de la calle.*'"

"And what does that mean?"

"It means 'my friend from the street.'"

"Good job," his mom said. "So go ahead and read it."

He unfolded the paper and stared at the letter. It had the same title in English.

"Why don't you read it out loud? Grandma and Grandpa know what this is all about, but they haven't read the note."

"Okay, Daddy. This is exciting, I think."

And then Remington read the note that would change part of his family's life for the next year and maybe even longer.

My friend from the street,
I thought you special in the street that night. I know you were good boy.

For years many I teach the children in my small town.

I know good children. I was professor.

That night you scared. That night you not like me. I know you look to me and be frightened boy.

I sorry I you make worried. I only want to help you.

You are lucky niño to be with parents and grandparents you have.

They want to help me, and I can you help. Listen to them.

If you me like, we be friends. More it is important, we be teacher and student.

Con abrazo,

Su amiga, María Rodríguez de Montón

When Remington was through reading the note, he just stood there staring at it for at least fifteen seconds. None of his family said anything. Finally, he looked up with a smile on his face. "I think I know who the note is from, but why is this a Christmas present?"

While he was reading the note, his parents had sat down on the sofa. They had left a space between them. "Come here and sit down," said his dad.

Remington walked across the room, but before he reached the sofa, he saw his grandmother standing by the room divider. She was wiping tears from her eyes with the beautiful embroidered handkerchief he had given her for Christmas. It was a late gift. He had found it while they were buying sweaters in Morella. "Grandma," he said with a smile on his face, "it looks like you are getting good use out of my Christmas gift."

Everyone laughed.

"We needed that laughter, Remington. We really should be very happy. Your grandma is crying because she is happy. I know; it's just the way grandmas are sometimes."

Remington's dad continued, "I think we are going to help someone who needs it and help you learn Spanish and even have a person living here who can help your mom with the apartment and with shopping and maybe"—he started laughing slightly—"and maybe even teach your mom how to say a few words."

"Real funny," said Remington's mom and playfully put an elbow against the ribs of her husband. "Here, Remington, sit."

Remington slid between them and listened as his dad told him about seeing the old homeless woman who had helped save Remington. He explained about her former life and all the bad things that had happened. When he was finished, he asked Remington, "Would you like to have her come here and teach us?"

Remington looked at him and said nothing.

"Well, would you?" His mom tapped him on the shoulder, and he turned to look at her. But there was nothing but a blank stare.

"What is it?"

"Mom, will she have those smelly clothes on?"

"Oh my gracious. Of course she won't. We have already bought her some new clothes. We have put her in a shelter for the homeless, and she is going to come live with us. There is so much room in the upstairs floor; she can have that whole floor, and you can have your own special room for learning Spanish."

"So what do you think now?" asked his dad.

Remington paused again. Mr. and Mrs. McGillicuddy walked to the front of the sofa. Four sets of eyes were on him. And then he surprised them all. He leaped to his feet, ran to the center of the room, and stopped with his back to the four of them.

"You mean you don't want her to come help you?"

"Oh, Grandma," he said and spun around on his toes. His heels fell back to the floor, and he had a big grin on his face. "Of course I want her to come. She's right. She was my friend that night. Without her and my buddy, Bobby, something bad might have happened to me.

"And most of all, you know what?" Remington paused but didn't give them time to answer. "I've learned you can't judge a book by its cover."

All five members of the family joined in a circle in the middle of the living room, and they hugged and cheered. Then Remington's dad strode off to finalize everything. After spending five minutes on the telephone, he came back into the living room. The other four looked at him. He waited a moment, and then he said, "It's done. We have a new nanny, a new teacher, and a new resident at twenty-five *Calle Fomento*."

"Oh, Richard, I am so happy," said Mrs. McGillicuddy.

"We are all happy," said Remington. "And I'm going to go tell Bobby."

"Well, make it quick. We've got the other big present to give out in just ten minutes."

"I'll be right back."

"Come on, Remington. We are waiting."

"You are certainly being mysterious, Lisa" said Mrs. McGillicuddy.

"Don't worry, Mom; it will be worth the wait."

"I can't imagine anything being better than these amazing three weeks here in Spain," said Mr. McGillicuddy.

"You might be surprised."

"Who's going to be surprised, Daddy?" Remington said as he skipped into the room.

"It's time for your grandparents' gift. Do you want to do the honors and present them like you did a year ago when we gave them the airline tickets?"

"Oh, yeah," said Remington, and a huge grin stretched across his face. It was so big that some of the freckles on his nose looked like they were going to pop off. "You are right. I am an expert at this."

"Now what have you got planned, you little trickster?"

"Just this," answered Remington, and he walked to the tall, deep brown armoire that sat in the corner of the room nearest the front door. He opened the top drawer and took something out. He walked back across the room and stood in front of the sofa.

"Close your eyes and hold out your hands."

"I remember something like this happening last Christmas," Mrs. McGillicuddy said.

"Well, you should, because it is almost the same thing." He put an envelope in each of their hands. "Open your eyes and take a look."

The two of them stared briefly at the envelopes. Mr. McGillicuddy tore his open first. "Oh my gosh! Is this what I think it is?"

"It is," Remington's mom said, "if you think it's an airline ticket so you can come back here for a special trip we are taking here in Spain next summer."

And then the hugs, the tears, the laughter, and the smiles made Christmas on January sixth in Madrid even better.

"I've got the best news ever!"

"What is it?" Bellowed Uncle Flicker. "Hopefully we aren't going to lie here, stretched from one end of the window sill to the other, until the McGillicuddys pack us up in the suitcase."

"No, but you are partly right. Remington got his folks to agree to keep the strand here on the windowsill, which means we won't be in a dark closet."

"But, why?"

"Perfect reason, Mom. The McGillicuddys are coming back for a summer visit and will take us with them when they return home. Remington is going to get to plug us in each night for a few minutes. Then on weekends, we can be turned on all the time whenever he is in the house."

In a matter of seconds the bulbs realized what Bobby had said, and they began to cheer excitedly.

"Oh, this is so wonderful," said Bobby's mom. "We can actually be together as one big family for more than just a few days. Two years ago was our greatest Christmas ever, Bobby, but this will be our greatest year ever."

Epilogue

It was six thirty on the morning of January seventh.

"I'm so tired, Mom."

"Well, I told you. I tried to get you to go to bed at nine o'clock last night because you had to get up early."

"I know," said Remington as he took the final bite from what had once been three scrambled eggs. "It's just that I wanted to stay up and play those games with Grandpa and Grandma. I am going to miss them so much."

"We will miss you even more," said Mrs. McGillicuddy.

Remington turned his head. "How long have you two been standing there?"

"Since you were about halfway through those eggs," answered Mr. McGillicuddy. "And the way you were eating them, that's only been about half a minute."

Remington laughed and quickly shoved the chair back from the table and ran to the doorway and hugged his grandparents.

"So, Lisa," Mrs. McGillicuddy asked, "you and Richard are taking Remington to school and then coming back to take us to the airport?"

"No, we are all going together to school, and then we will go on to the airport. That way you get a few more minutes with Remington."

"Remington, you have to promise us you will take care of our miracle bulbs. Are you sure we shouldn't just take them with us to make sure they are safe?"

"No, Grandpa, you don't mean it, do you?"

"Just kidding, good buddy." A big grin broke out on Mr. McGillicuddy's face.

"Good, because while you're back in America, I'm going to teach Bobby how to say not only his name but also my name and even John and Jane."

Mr. and Mrs. McGillicuddy started laughing, but Remington's mom frowned and said, "Oh, Remington! Please, you are not going to make me believe a bulb can talk."

"Don't be so sure. He has said his name at least three times."

"No, you think you heard a noise that sounded like the word *Bobby*."

"Oh, don't be too sure, Lisa," Mr. McGillicuddy interrupted. "I've got an idea." There was a strange look on his face.

"When you raise your eyebrows like that, John McGillicuddy," his wife said, "you are being mischievous. What are you talking about?"

"Remington,"—he peered down at his grandson who was now standing near the kitchen table—"if you are going to teach Bobby some new words, why don't you have him teach you some words in his language?"

"That's a great idea." Remington started jumping up and down. "I never thought of it. Maybe Bobby and all those bulbs do have their own language."

Remington started giggling. "What do you think they speak, Grandpa?"

Mr. McGillicuddy raised his eyebrows again, and with a big smile on his face, he looked at Remington. Out of the corner of his eye he could see his daughter-in-law and his wife looking at him.

"You, know, I wouldn't be surprised if those bulbs speak *Bulbese*."

John Brooks is a semi-retired sportscaster, hall of fame broadcaster, and owner of Sportscast Productions, Inc, a radio and television sports production and sports advertising company. With nearly 3,300 professional and collegiate play-by-play broadcasts on his resume, his many credits include sixteen years as Voice of the University of Oklahoma Football and Basketball radio networks, two years as Voice of the Tulsa University Basketball and Football radio networks, and the Voice of the Oklahoma City Blazers and San Diego Gulls professional hockey teams for twenty-eight years. He is married to Lisa, has three children, Remington, Stacey, and Angie, and lives in Oklahoma City and part-time in Madrid, Spain.

Other Bobby Bright Books:
"Bobby Bright's Greatest Christmas Ever"
"Bobby Bright's Christmas Heroics"
"Bobby Bright Becomes a Professor"
"Bobby Bright Meets His Maker"